A Dream of
Queens
and Castles

Also by Marion Dane Bauer

Touch the Moon
On My Honor
Like Mother, Like Daughter
Rain of Fire
Tangled Butterfly
Foster Child
Shelter from the Wind

MARION DANE BAUER

A Dream of Queens and Castles

CLARION BOOKS ❋ NEW YORK

Acknowledgments

Special thanks to Kathleen Tripp and Janet Miles, who
blessed England for me, and to the Reverend Marilyn
Beckstrom and the Tuesday Night Writers, who blessed
my homecoming.
And appreciation, too, to the Reverend Frederick .
William Nairn and to my stepfather, William Barker, my
experts on British customs and speech.

Clarion Books
a Houghton Mifflin Company imprint
215 Park Avenue South, New York, NY 10003
Text copyright © 1990 by Marion Dane Bauer
All rights reserved.

For information about permission to reproduce
selections from this book, write to Permissions,
Houghton Mifflin Company, 2 Park Street, Boston, MA 02018.
Printed in the USA

Bauer, Marion Dane.
A dream of queens and castles / Marion Dane Bauer.
    p.   cm.
Summary: In England with her mother for a year, dreamy Diana meets
an eccentric old man and shares his frustrations and use of the
royal family as a means of escape.
ISBN 0-395-51330-8
[1. England—Fiction. 2. Kings, queens, rulers, etc.—Fiction.
3. Friendship—Fiction.]   I. Title.
[PZ7.B3262Dr   1990]
[Fic]—dc20   89-17400
                                                      CIP
                                                       AC

BP 10 9 8 7 6 5 4 3 2 1

For Annie,
who shares my every dream

A Dream of
Queens
and Castles

1

DIANA STOOD first on one foot, then on the other. The line seemed to be barely moving. It had been bad enough to spend twelve hours flying from Minneapolis to England, and now that they were here, it was taking forever to get through customs.

If Princess Di knew that her American namesake was being treated so discourteously, she would be furious. The dungeon would be too good for these petty officials who allowed Diana Baldwin from Minnesota to stand in line.

Diana felt a nudge from behind. "You're dreaming again, sweetie," her mother said. "Better keep moving with the line."

"I'm not dreaming," Diana said, defending herself automatically. She picked up her carry-on bag, moved several steps forward, and plopped it down again . . . hard.

Her mother didn't understand. She didn't understand much of anything these days. She certainly didn't understand about dreams. If Diana dreamed about boys, her mother said twelve was too young for such things. If she dreamed about queens and castles,

Mom told her it was time to grow up. Some people never could make up their minds.

Diana turned back to her mother. After all, she had no one else to talk to in this strange country. "Do you suppose he'll notice?" she asked.

"He? Who? Notice what?" Her mother studied her, her gray eyes puzzled.

"Him. The man in customs. Do you suppose he'll notice my name?"

"What about your name?" Mom reached out to push a strand of hair away from Diana's face.

Diana flipped her head so the hair fell back into place again. "That it's the same as *hers* . . . Princess Di's."

"Oh." Her mother laughed, a deep, throaty laugh Diana had loved once. Now the sound of it ran beneath her skin like an itch. "Probably not. The people in customs have more important things to think about."

More important than Princess Di, the next Queen of England? Diana found that hard to believe. She turned her back on her mother and resumed waiting.

Princess Di would understand about dreams. Anybody who married a prince and got turned into a princess would have to understand about dreams. She would understand, too, how Diana felt about leaving her friends, moving to a strange place, starting over for what felt like the millionth time. Diana had read an article once about how hard it had been for Princess Di at first, leaving her old life behind to move into the palace. Sometimes, the article had said, the Princess even cried.

It'll be great. You'll see, her mother had said, also for what felt like the millionth time. But it wouldn't. Nothing about it would be great.

It's only for a year, her mother had reminded her every time she had complained, *and then we'll be going back to Minneapolis*. But a year was forever. A year was enough time to shrivel and die. It was certainly enough time for people to forget they had ever known you. Even Meghan, Diana's best friend, would probably forget her in that amount of time.

Besides, Diana remembered too well what it had been like making friends when she had moved to Minneapolis two years before . . . and to Denver before that and to Fort Worth before that.

In the beginning everybody had treated her like a visitor from another planet. And wouldn't it be ten times worse when you moved, not just to another city in another state, but to another country? It wasn't as if she was a little kid any longer, the dumb little kid who didn't care where she was as long as she was with her mommy.

Her mother touched her shoulder once more, and Diana moved forward without waiting for the inevitable orders. That was all she got these days, orders. Do this, do that, go here, stay there! She had never before wished so ardently to be grown and in charge of her own life.

When she was grown she wouldn't ever move again

as long as she lived. Her mother could go on moving, since she liked it so much. Diana wouldn't even leave Minneapolis to go visiting. Mom could be the one to travel to her.

"Next," the customs official said, and Diana picked up her carry-on bag before her mother could nudge her again. She moved toward the customs station, her mother following as if she had been the one called. But of course that is the way it would be. Diana didn't even have her own passport. She was listed on her mother's, as though she wasn't even a separate person.

The man opened the passport and studied it with a bored expression. His face was red. Perhaps his collar was too tight.

"Name?" he asked in a crisp voice without looking up to indicate which one of them he was speaking to.

"Kathleen Baldwin," her mother replied.

Diana said nothing. The man didn't even notice.

"Occupation?"

"Professor of English literature," Mom told him.

Diana pressed her lips together and gazed off across the cavernous room. What occupation did she have anyway, except following her mother around the world?

"Length of stay?"

Too long, Diana thought. But her mother answered, "Until June nineteen eighty-nine."

"Purpose?" He still wasn't looking at either of them.

"We're going to visit the royal family," Diana said, though she hadn't really intended to speak.

But her mother said quickly, almost on top of her, "I'm on an exchange with an instructor from Bishop Grossteste College in Lincoln."

The customs official looked up slowly, not at Diana's mother, but at her. "So you're going to meet the Queen, are you?" His expression bordered on friendliness.

Diana shook her head. She could feel herself blushing. "No . . . Princess Di."

The man looked down at the open passport and then at her again. "Well, miss," he said, as he stamped the small navy book with a resounding thump, "I'm sure Lady Diana will be proud to have a visit from an American lass with such a fine name."

Diana looked her mother straight in the eye. *See*, she said, speaking without words the way they had always been able to do. *He noticed*.

But her mother made no response. She merely motioned for Diana to take charge of the carry-on bags and started toward the carousel where the rest of the luggage was parading around and around.

Diana picked up the two smaller suitcases and followed. What else could she do? When you were a kid and your mother decided you were going to move to England, you moved.

But still, her heart was beating a hopeful tattoo. Princess Diana was going to be "proud to have a visit from an American lass with such a fine name." Lady Diana, the man had called her, but she really was a princess.

Diana could see the scenario as clearly as she could see her mother's retreating back. All she had to do was stop by Buckingham Palace and give one of the guards her name. He would pass the word inside.

"A lass named Diana to see the Princess," and Lady Di would hurry out to meet her.

No, she would invite Diana in . . . into the palace, into her royal chambers even. Once she was there, Diana would tell Lady Di everything about herself. And Lady Di would listen. She would listen and she would look at Diana in the special way of someone who really sees what she is looking at. And then she would say, "I understand. Of course. I understand exactly how you feel."

She would sit Diana down and ring for a servant to bring her something to eat. Tea and crumpets maybe, whatever crumpets were. Then she would say, "You want to go home? Why, let me . . ."

Mom reappeared lugging two large suitcases. "Can you manage the carry-ons?" she asked. She was looking frazzled and tired. "The train to London isn't very far."

"Of course," Diana said, suffused with a sudden new energy. Maybe they weren't going to be staying in England so long, after all. "Are you sure those big ones aren't too heavy?" She smiled at her mother to let her see how grown up she was, how ready to be responsible for her part of the load.

Her mother smiled back, clearly surprised and pleased. "Thanks for asking," she said, "but I can manage."

The train to London. Diana fell into step beside her, moving willingly for the first time since they had left their house the day before. After all, Buckingham Palace was in London.

And when they got there, Diana thought she just might introduce her mom to Lady Di.

*

The door of the underground train rumbled shut, and Diana edged through the crowd, dropping her suitcases onto the dirty, metal floor. She didn't even glance back to see if her mother had made it on with the larger ones.

It was so unfair! Here they were passing right through London — well, beneath London, which was practically the same thing — and her mother had refused to stop anywhere even for a short while. When Diana had mentioned Buckingham Palace she had merely shaken her head and answered, "We're too tired to manage any excursions now." (That's what she had said, *we*, as if Diana was obligated to be tired because she was.)

In fact, her mother had refused even to take a taxi so that they might have had a chance to drive by something (or someone) interesting. *Too expensive*, she had said, *and too slow.* So here they were taking this crowded, noisy underground train directly to Kings Cross Station on the other side of the city. And once there, they would take another surface train to Lincoln without making a single stop. The only thing her mother cared about was getting to Coleby, the little village outside of Lincoln where they were renting a house, and then, of course, getting to work the next day. The only thing she had ever cared about for Diana's entire life was getting to work.

We'll come back, her mother had promised. *We'll see the Tower of London, museums, parks. We'll even see the changing of the guard at Buckingham Palace.* But Diana didn't want to come back, and she didn't care about the Tower of London or museums or parks. She didn't even care about the guard at Buckingham Palace, whether it changed or not. She just wanted to meet Lady Di. Was that too much to ask? She wanted to meet Lady Di, and she wanted to go home.

The train lurched into motion, and Diana had to grab for a pole to keep from toppling over. Not that she would have toppled very far. She was wedged so tightly into a pack of other morning travelers — morning in London but still the middle of the night by Minnesota time — that she couldn't have fallen to the floor if she had wanted to.

A tall teenage boy moved in next to Diana, and she had to look away to keep from staring. The sides of the boy's head were shaved, and the hair on top, colored in alternating bands of shocking pink and chartreuse, stood in a tall, spiky ridge. He had huge safety pins sticking through his ears, too, like earrings, and he had on a leather vest without a shirt.

The bare shoulder nearest Diana bulged under what appeared to be a tattoo of a naked woman. She had averted her eyes so quickly that she hadn't seen it very clearly, but she was pretty certain that was what it was. She kept wanting to look again, to inspect the tattoo more closely, but the nakedness of the woman embarrassed her. Besides, she didn't want to be caught staring. The punker looked tough.

The train, which had been rocketing through a dark tunnel, began to slow as it came into the more open, lighted area of another station. Diana leaned forward to look around the boy. As annoyed with her mother as she was, she couldn't help being relieved to find her standing there, just inside the door.

"Is this where we're supposed to get off?" she mouthed over the din of the train.

Her mother shook her head, and Diana straightened up again.

The train jerked to a stop. People pushed past them, first leaving, then entering the car. In the brief clearing Diana picked up her suitcases and moved a few steps down the aisle . . . away from the safety pins and the tattoo. Away from her mother, too, for that matter.

The train started up again, the last passengers barely getting on before the double doors chomped shut like the jaws of a hungry monster. Diana settled into the clacking, rattling rhythm of the movement.

The underground train stopped and started, stopped and started again. Each time they arrived at a station Diana glanced back at her mother, and each time Mom shook her head and smiled — a bit wearily, but still a smile. Her mother looked vulnerable, somehow, as though she had grown smaller during the flight. For a moment, Diana almost wanted to reach out to touch her.

It's all right, she would say. *It's all right if we don't stop at Buckingham Palace just yet.*

She had moved too far away to reach, though. And besides, the punker was still between them.

Diana studied the map of the underground on the wall. It was a skein of different colored threads criss-crossing beneath the city. Too bad they didn't make the trains and the tunnels the same color they were on the maps. That way they would be riding on a blue train through a blue tunnel.

She could suggest it when she met Lady Di. A bit of color would improve this underground system immeasurably.

Diana repeated to herself for probably the hundredth time, *an American lass with such a fine name*, savoring the old-fashioned-sounding word, *lass*.

Would an American lass who found herself a prince have a chance to become a princess, too?

"Your Royal Highness," everyone would say, and the women would all curtsy . . . even Diana's mother would have to curtsy. Because her mother wouldn't be royalty. To be royalty you either had to be born to it or you had to marry into it, and her mother wasn't about to marry anyone, not even a prince.

Not since she had divorced Diana's father, and she had done that when Diana was just a tiny baby, before Diana had even had a chance to meet him properly.

"Diana."

Diana heard her name above the din, and she gave a nod in her mother's direction without really looking. How could her mother tell she was dreaming from so far away, anyway?

Maybe her father had been a dreamer, too. Maybe that had been why —

"Diana!" This time the voice penetrated Diana's reverie, and she turned to look. Her mother was standing on the station platform, a suitcase in each hand, seeming to reach with her chin toward the train door. "Diana, I told you it was time —"

The doors began to slide closed, and her mother dropped her suitcases and leaped toward the train. Even as she leaped, though, the doors clanked shut. Instantly, the train jerked, then started forward again.

Diana watched, immobilized, as her mother ran along beside the train shouting something she couldn't hear. She could see her mouth move, that was all.

And then the train plunged into the dark tunnel, and her mother was gone.

2

DIANA CAME alive at last, gasping. She lunged for the door and banged on it. "Stop!" she shouted. "Please, stop!" But the train was already going full speed, and it showed no signs of stopping.

She burst into tears. Here she was, lost beneath London, and she would never see her mother, never see anyone familiar again! She had known something terrible would happen if they moved to this place.

All over the lighted car, people were turning to look at her, curiosity mingled with pity. Diana covered her face with one arm, wishing she could vanish. She didn't know why she so often imagined situations where people were watching her. But when something actually happened and people looked, it never felt the way it was supposed to.

"Say there, darling." The punker put a hand on her shoulder. "Don't get your knickers in a twist. It'll be all right."

Don't get your knickers in a twist? Diana whirled to confront the wild hair and the stupid safety pins.

What kind of an idiot would put safety pins in his ears, anyway? "How? How is it going to be all right? That's my mom back there. She'll never see me again!" And her tears flowed anew.

"Of course she will. I'll show you what to do."

Diana snorted and scrubbed at her tears, glaring at the boy. "What?" she demanded, not caring how rude she sounded. "What can I do?"

He bent over her so that his face came close to hers and spoke in a low voice — as low as anybody could over the rumbling of the train. "You just get out at the next stop and stand there on the platform, right at the front where your mum will see you when she comes. She'll take the next train. It'll only be five minutes . . . ten at the most, and she'll catch you up again."

Diana sniffed, nodded, tried to smile. She felt like an idiot, a baby and an idiot, first not paying attention to where she was supposed to get off and then sniveling like this.

"Thanks," she muttered, not really looking at the boy.

"Don't mention it. In fact, I'll get off and wait with you just to make sure you get found."

"Oh, you don't need — " Diana started to say, but then she felt the train braking. She had a sudden vision of herself standing, entirely alone, in the middle of a strange underground station, and she said instead, "That would be very nice. Thank you."

Diana and the boy disembarked when the train stopped, and he took up a position in the middle of the platform, back just a few feet from the tracks. The other people from the train flowed behind them and out, while those who had been standing on the platform charged on board. And the train disappeared into the tunnel, leaving behind only a momentary gust of cool air.

Diana set her suitcases down and waited, acutely aware of the tattoo on the shoulder next to her and the muscles rippling beneath it. She still was afraid to look at it directly, though.

When the rumbling of the metal wheels had died, the dingy platform was utterly still. Diana tried to think of something to say to break the silence. She studied her escort out of the corner of her eye. Weren't a lot of punk kids freaked out on drugs? And didn't drugs make people dangerous?

A deserted underground platform would be the perfect place for a murder. A person didn't have to know much about England to figure that out.

"Where do you come from?" the murderer asked politely. It was, Diana was certain, false politeness intended to put a victim off guard.

"Uh . . . Minnesota," she replied, moving her suitcases and herself a few inches back as inconspicuously as possible. If she screamed, would anybody hear her?

"That's in the States, right?"

"Right," Diana answered, taking another step.

"New York or California?" the boy asked, as if everything were one place or the other.

"Neither." What kind of a weapon would he use? The giant safety pins? No, that was silly. All he would need to do would be to push her in front of the next train. And when the authorities found her mangled corpse, they wouldn't know what to do with it. She would be buried anonymously in a pauper's grave, and her mother would spend the rest of her life wondering what had happened to her and being sorry she had insisted on moving again. "It's in the middle and north," she said, "just below Canada."

Diana took another step backward, leaving the suitcases this time. They were the least of her concerns.

"Gor blimey!" The boy glanced down at the distance widening between them without seeming to see it. "Near Canada? Do you ever have summer there?"

Diana laughed, but she didn't forget to take another step. "Of course. It gets to be over a hundred degrees sometimes . . . Fahrenheit," she added, remembering that her mother had said they used centigrade here and that one hundred degrees centigrade was the point at which water boiled.

People were trickling onto the station platform. Maybe she would be safe now. At least there would be witnesses if she died, someone to tell her mother exactly what had happened after she had abandoned her to her fate.

"A hundred degrees," the boy repeated wonderingly, and he turned and walked toward her, closing in two steps the distance she had created with all her effort. "You'd better stay at the front. Your mum will be able to see you better there."

"Oh." Diana tried to look startled, as if the platform had been moving, not she. "Of course." She moved forward again, picking up her suitcases and positioning herself as far back from the concrete trench that held the tracks as she thought could still qualify for being at the front.

The boy followed and stationed himself next to her once more. "How long have you been over here?" he asked.

"I just arrived," she replied coolly, looking toward the dark tunnel from which the next train would appear. And then she added in a flash of inspiration, "I'm on my way to see Lady Di." Surely no British citizen, not even a punker, would interfere with someone on such an important mission.

"Oh," the boy said, apparently as impressed as she had meant for him to be. "By invitation?"

Diana looked up to see if he was making fun of her, but there wasn't even a trace of a smile around his mouth or in his eyes. If fact, he looked quite interested and, despite his strange hair and fierce dress, even gentle somehow.

And to her own surprise, she found herself telling the truth. "Not exactly by invitation. I just want to see her. That's all. In fact," she added with a sudden passion that surprised even her, "I need to see her real bad. She's the only one who can help me."

"Are you in some kind of trouble, then?"

Diana nodded, embarrassed to find her throat suddenly closing and her mouth twitching downward at the corners in preparation for more tears.

But the boy didn't make matters worse by pushing more questions at her the way so many adults would have. He merely waited, discreetly studying an advertisement on the opposite tunnel wall, until she could speak. When she started, the words tumbled out without further encouragement.

"My mother doesn't understand. She doesn't even try. She thinks nothing matters except her job. Not me. Not my friends. She made me come here, you know. I didn't want to, but she made me." Again Diana stopped, struggling against the maddening tears. She didn't know where they were coming from. She had cried and cried before they had left home, but she had been certain by the time they walked onto the plane that she was through with all that. After all, the crying hadn't done a bit of good.

"And Lady Di?" the boy inquired in a puzzled but kindly voice.

Lady Di? The name echoed in Diana's mind. How could she explain? Anything she said would sound dumb.

"I just thought . . ." She took a deep, wavery breath. "We share a name, you know. She and I. I'm Diana, too. She seems so nice, when you see her in photos, I mean, and when you read about her."

Diana was watching the punker out of the corner of her eye as she spoke, waiting for a sneer or even a superior, adult kind of smile. Neither one came. He was listening, seriously, with all his attention.

"I want," she said. "I want . . ." And then it occurred to her in a rush exactly what she wanted. She wanted someone, someone exactly like Lady Di, to see her, to know that she was alive, that she mattered. To simply look at her and read the deepest secrets unfolding inside of her. But of course, she couldn't say any of that, so she said instead, rather lamely, "I want to tell Lady Di about my dreams."

The boy nodded his tall ridge of pink and chartreuse hair and said, solemnly, "I think the Princess would like that. She's one who knows about girls' dreams."

Diana turned to stare at him, her mouth dropping open of its own weight. But before she could think of anything further to say, a train came blasting out of the tunnel, stopping all possibility for conversation with its noise. And then her mother was stepping onto the platform, her face tinged gray and her features out of alignment somehow.

"Thanks!" Diana shouted over the din. "Thanks ever so much. I've got to go now. I see my mom over there." She held out her hand, and the boy took it. And now she could see the tattoo clearly for the first time. It wasn't a naked woman at all. It was a mermaid. Only half a naked woman. And quite beautiful, too.

Her hand still warm from the boy's grip, she picked up her suitcases and hurried toward her mother, who had spotted her and was also hurrying, almost running despite her own heavy luggage.

But even as Diana steeled herself against the scolding she could see gathering in her mother's eyes, her heart sang. It didn't matter if her mother was cross. It didn't matter at all. She, Diana, was going to meet the next Queen of England.

And most important of all, the next Queen of England was going to meet her.

3

DIANA LOOKED at her fried eggs with distaste. The yolks were dark orange. She put her fork down and gazed instead at a patch of early morning sky visible through one of the windows of the ancient stone cottage that was to be their home for the next year. The sky was the same color as the lead divisions between the panes of wavy glass. She didn't know what she had expected, but she certainly hadn't expected everything in England to be so old and so gray.

Diana's mother came bustling in, the swinging door from the kitchen flapping closed and open and closed again behind her. She was apparently already over her jet lag, but then she always got over whatever was bothering her when it was time to go to work.

"Haven't you finished your breakfast yet? We'll be late. The bus to Lincoln leaves at eight-thirty."

Diana picked up her toast and dipped a point into the garish yolk. She nibbled at the toast with her front teeth, rabbit style — her mother couldn't stand to see her eat that way — before replying. "What do you mean, *we'll* be late. *I* don't have anywhere to go."

"Diana, I have to be in Lincoln this morning" — her

mother was steadfastly ignoring the way she was eating — "to meet the people I'll be working with. I told
you that. I wish you would listen."

"I listen. I know exactly what you told me. But
you're the one who's going to be working with those
people, not me. There's no reason for me to go."
Diana set the toast down and wiped her hands on her
jeans. The toast was tough, anyway. She liked soft
toast, barely golden, made from what her mother dis-
dainfully called "squishy white bread." Apparently
the English didn't even know how to make soft bread.

Her mother sighed, a long sigh that whistled
through her nose, and the sound drew a sudden heat
to Diana's face. Sighing was so unfair. It was a kind of
weapon her mother used, a way to make her feel bad
without a single word being uttered.

Mom spoke in the too-patient voice that went with
the sigh. "Sweetheart, you know I can't go off and
leave you alone . . . in a strange country . . . our first
full day here." She punctuated her sentence with a
smile that was supposed to make up for forcing Diana
to follow her around all day.

But it didn't. There was a time when Diana had liked
nothing better than going to work with her mother,
being patted on the head, listening to the respectful
way people said "Professor" or "Dr. Baldwin." But she
was too old for that now, much too old.

"Why can't you leave me here? I stay alone at home
. . . all the time."

"Not all the time," her mother corrected. "Just

sometimes. And when you stay alone at home you always have Meghan's mother to check in with. We don't know anybody in the village yet."

"Please, Mom. I'm responsible. Besides, it's boring, going to work with you. It's bad enough to have to move here, but if you're going to treat me like a baby . . ." She could hear a whine creeping into her voice and she let up abruptly. Her mother hated whining.

Mom frowned and checked her watch. Time was on Diana's side, she could tell. "Well, as to your being responsible, we didn't exactly get off to a good start yesterday with you lost on the underground."

"I wasn't lost," Diana shot back. "I was just separated from you. I knew where I was the entire time."

"And where were you? Making friends with a punker? That didn't exactly show a lot of discretion, you know."

Diana balled up her paper napkin and threw it on top of the staring eggs, grown cold and greasy on her plate. "He was nice," she said between clenched teeth. And then she added, but under her breath, "Just because you don't like men . . ."

It wasn't a fair thing to say, really. It wasn't even particularly true. Her mother had lots of friends, people she taught with, who were men, not to mention the ones she dated from time to time, when she wasn't too busy or too tired. But when it came right down to it, her mother didn't seem to *need* a man in her life . . . and Diana did.

Whether or not her mother heard the remark, she seemed to comprehend the territory they were in. Her arms had been crossed firmly over her chest, and she let them fall to her sides. It was an argument neither of them had ever won, the one about their not being a real family because there was no husband, no father. Her mother always insisted that they made a fine family, just the two of them, that they didn't need anybody more. Diana thought, and occasionally said, that the very least her mother could do would be to find her a father.

"All right, Diana. I suppose it isn't fair to expect you to trail after me." The resignation in her mother's voice almost made Diana feel guilty about having won. "But what will you do here all day long? There isn't even a shop of any description in Coleby . . . except for the two pubs, and you can't go there."

Diana shrugged. "I brought some books, and there's always TV." She nodded toward the living room where the TV set loomed incongruously next to an old-fashioned potbelly stove. The stove was apparently what they would be using to warm the living room in the winter. "Besides, I've got plans to make." And that wasn't a lie. She needed to spend some time thinking about what she was going to say when she met Lady Di.

At the word *plans* her mother narrowed her eyes suspiciously, but she said only, "I guess it'll be all right. Certainly, there isn't much trouble you could get into in a village as small as this one."

Diana's back stiffened. As if she always got into trouble when she was left alone!

Her mother, though, went on talking without seeming to notice that she had given any offense. "I'll leave the number of the college by the phone. You can call if you need anything. There's plenty of food in the refrigerator, of course. It's a good thing we shopped in Lincoln yesterday. And I'll be home on the bus that gets to Coleby at five-thirty."

It's not home, Diana thought, looking at her plate to avoid sending any further challenge. She could feel the weight of her mother's gaze settling on her.

"Do you want to walk me to the bus?"

Diana shrugged. "I guess so," she said, none too graciously. Then she looked up, remembering that she had been the victor in this small battle, and added, more cheerfully, "I'll come to meet you when you get back, too."

Her mother smiled wanly. She reached to pick up Diana's plate, but hesitated with her hand still in mid-air, her forehead rumpled. "Is this all you're going to eat?"

"I'm not hungry," Diana said, and her mother sighed again as she gathered up the dishes. At least she didn't go through her usual lecture on nutrition and on breakfast being the most important meal of the day.

"I'll be ready to go in a few minutes" was all she said, and she started toward the swinging door into the kitchen.

Diana called after her, "When will we be going back to London?"

"Back to London?" Mom caught the door with her shoulder. "Why do you want to do that?" As though she didn't know. But then she took a closer look at Diana's face and apparently remembered. "Oh," she said. "That."

"Yes," Diana replied, imitating her mother's tone. "That."

Mom sighed yet again. Someday Diana was going to start keeping track of how many times a day she did that. "I'll take you to London as soon as I have time, Diana. I'll even go stand outside Buckingham Palace with you, if that's what you want to do. But I'm afraid you're in for a disappointment. Members of the royal family don't spend their days running out to meet visitors."

Diana brushed the toast crumbs left on the polished wooden surface of the table into a small pile, scooping them together with the side of her hand.

"And the truth is" — her mother was backing through the door as she spoke — "the royal family and those they marry are just people like you and me. They have less freedom than we do, and a lot less privacy, but — " The rest of her words were cut off as the swinging door flapped shut behind her.

"Nobody has less freedom than I do," Diana said to the pile of crumbs, just before she brushed it off onto the floor.

For a moment she contemplated standing outside Buckingham Palace, her mother at her side, waiting to meet Lady Di.

It would never do. Her mother's very doubts would keep Lady Di away. It was as though Mom had already managed to defeat her, even when she was trying to help. And if they did get to meet Lady Di, her mother would probably do all the talking. Naturally, she would have to tell the Princess about her new job.

Maybe there was nothing Diana could do about having to move here in the first place, and maybe it wasn't sensible to count on Lady Di to be able to send her home. But there was one thing Diana could take charge of . . . and would.

She was going to visit Buckingham Palace, and somehow she was going to go there on her own.

4

DIANA'S MOTHER chose a seat in the lower part of the double-decker bus and leaned toward the mud-spattered window to wave. Diana waved back, wondering why anyone would settle for a ride in the bottom of the bus. Yesterday when they had ridden the bus together, Diana had taken them to the upper level. People were allowed to smoke up there, and Mom didn't like smoke, but what was a little smoke in exchange for a more interesting ride?

Her mother was smiling, but even the smile was a bit dubious, as though she might suddenly decide to throw open the window and insist that Diana get on the bus and come to Lincoln with her.

Diana waved once more, turned away, and began walking briskly back along the quiet, cobbled street toward the village. She wasn't about to risk any change of heart . . . Mom's or her own.

She rarely had trouble finding things to do, anyway. If she had been home she wouldn't have thought twice about being alone on a long summer's day. Though if she were home, she would have friends to do things with. Meghan and Julie and . . .

What would Meghan and Julie be doing today? They

had probably decided the moment Diana left to take that stuck-up Pam into their group. And by the time Diana got home again the three of them would be attached like glue. There wouldn't be any room for her. Pam had never liked Diana anyway, and she would probably talk the others out of being her friend as well.

Diana kept walking. She wrapped her arms around herself and shivered. She was wearing jeans and a sweatshirt, but despite its being late June, the morning was raw. She couldn't see why the punker had asked if it ever got to be summer in Minnesota. As far as she could tell, it never got to be summer here.

Maybe she should go back to bed. It was barely eight-thirty. As boring as Coleby looked to be, she would probably spend a lot of time in bed this next year. If her mother had to move her to England, the least she could have done would be to pick some place interesting . . . like London. Near Buckingham Palace, maybe.

Diana took a deep breath. She had plans to make . . . for getting to Buckingham Palace without her mother in tow. She had to learn the lay of the land, get her mother to give her some English money, all those kinds of things. In the meantime, though, she might as well explore this cold, damp little village. It wouldn't take her long, and then she could go to bed and stay there for the rest of the day, thinking. Except that she would get up to meet her mother's bus, show her how responsible she was, let her see that she could take care of herself, even in this foreign place.

Coleby didn't take long to explore. It had two pubs, as her mother had said. It also had a hole-in-the-wall post office, a tiny, ramshackle school, and a church, as dark and as damp-smelling inside as a tomb. And of course, there were houses. Most of them looked as ancient as the three-hundred-year-old stone cottage she and her mother were renting. Even what must have been newer homes were built to look old, though Diana couldn't understand why.

At least the school wasn't the one she would be attending in the fall. Her mother had explained that kids in the seventh grade went to a larger school in a village nearby. Only here her grade would be called the "first form."

Diana paused at the entrance to a path that seemed to lead out of town. There was a symbol of a Viking helmet on a post to mark it. She recognized it as a Viking helmet because of the Minnesota Vikings, the football team. This presumably referred to the real thing, the Vikings who had invaded Britain centuries before, though why the English people wanted to honor invaders by naming a path after them she couldn't figure. Maybe just as everyone thought people grew more important by getting older, even invaders got to be heroes after the invasion became ancient enough.

Diana decided to follow the footpath a ways. She had seen all there was to see in the village, and she wasn't sleepy any longer.

The path, to begin with, passed between two yards — gardens, her mother had told her they would be called here — set off by a tall hedge on one side and an ivy-strewn wall on the other. Beyond the gardens was a stile, wooden steps that climbed a stone wall and then went down the other side into a pasture. There were cattle grazing in the pasture, and Diana hesitated at the top of the stile. The animals seemed to pay no attention to her, though, so she stepped down.

The path followed a ridge overlooking an expanse of flat, green fields little different from those she was used to seeing in Minnesota. More green perhaps, a vibrant, shimmering green even on such a dull day, but nothing special.

Still she kept on going. At least walking was something to do. Besides, who could tell? Maybe this Viking trail went all the way to London. If she had enough supplies, she might be able to walk that far. Not today, but some day soon.

Maybe she should write a letter to Lady Di first so the Princess would be expecting her. That was something she could do today.

Halfway across the pasture, Diana hesitated. An old man was approaching on the path, apparently returning to the village after a walk. A girl who looked to be about Diana's age was beside him, probably his granddaughter. The man's upper back was bent like a question mark, and he moved tentatively, as if testing the ground before placing each foot. It was difficult to tell if he was escorting the girl or she him.

In any case, the two were deep in conversation, and neither of them glanced up to see Diana. She considered turning around, climbing the stile and hurrying back into the village, but she didn't. She had as much right to be on a public path as they did, didn't she?

She resumed walking. Maybe it would be a chance to meet the girl.

The girl looked up then, caught sight of Diana and immediately looked down again . . . as if she had no interest in meeting someone new. The girl belonged here, no doubt. She probably lived in Coleby and took a walk with her grandfather every morning. Why would she want to meet a stranger, a foreigner?

Again Diana had an impulse to turn back, but she was drawing too close now. To walk right up to these people and then to turn around and walk back to the village immediately in front of them would look weird. She wouldn't speak to them when they passed, though. At least she wouldn't speak unless one of them spoke first.

As she drew abreast of the pair, the old man looked up, fixing his milky, blue gaze on Diana. "Well, good morning," he boomed. "And who might you be?"

The deep voice coming from the ancient little man startled Diana into a sudden halt. She stared at him as if she hadn't known he was there. "Di-Diana, sir," she stuttered. "Diana Baldwin from Minnesota."

He had a great shock of white hair and white, bushy eyebrows that met to form a kind of shelf above his pale eyes. He nodded approvingly, as if his question had been a kind of test and she had passed with flying colors.

"Excellent," he said. "Excellent. We are honored to meet you, Diana-Baldwin-from-Minnesota." He ran it together as if it were all her name.

Diana turned to see if the old man's enthusiasm at meeting her was shared, but the girl looked back with a blankness so complete that it bordered on hostility. Instead of speaking to Diana she tugged on her companion's sleeve. "Come along, Granddad," she commanded. "You've got to get on home so I can go to school."

School! Diana gaped. Surely no civilized country kept kids in school this far into the summer.

But the old man shook off his granddaughter's hold. "If it's late that worries you, Elspeth, why don't you run on? I'll not have any trouble finding my way home." As he spoke he winked and smiled at Diana, his face gathering into a mass of friendly wrinkles. Diana found herself smiling, too, though she wasn't sure what she was smiling about.

Elspeth remained serious, however . . . and immovable. "Mum said I was to bring you back," she objected, her fists cocked on her narrow hips.

Diana stood watching the exchange, not involved particularly, just watching, until the old man surprised her by nodding in her direction and saying, "This good lady will bring me back. Won't you?"

Diana looked around quickly to find what lady he meant before she realized, with a stab of pleasurable embarrassment, that he was speaking of her.

Elspeth didn't even glance in Diana's direction. "Mum said — " she began.

"Mum said, Mum said," the old man snorted. "Am I to do everything your *mum* says, then?"

Diana was fascinated. She sympathized with the girl's obvious frustration, but the old man's struggle with Elspeth's "mum" rather reminded her of her own with her mother. Besides, she liked his spirit.

Elspeth answered with the careful articulation of one who has lost all patience but is struggling to be polite. "Granddad, this girl doesn't even know you. She doesn't want to bring you home. Now, please — "

"Of course I do," Diana interrupted before she even knew she was going to speak. "Does your grandpa live in Coleby? I'd be glad to walk him home."

She didn't know why she had said it exactly, except that he seemed to be such a nice old man. Besides, she had always wanted a grandfather of her own. That was another thing her mother had cheated her out of. Her mother's own father had died before Diana was born, and though her father's parents faithfully sent Diana gifts for birthdays and Christmas — for her twelfth birthday a baby doll and a Donald Duck hat from Disney World — Diana hadn't seen either of them for years. With all her mother's moving around, her grandparents had never gotten a chance to know her properly, or she them. So it was little wonder they didn't know what kinds of presents to send.

The old man's eyes shone when he looked at Diana, and she was glad she had made the offer.

"There now," he said to Elspeth. "Go along with you. Diana here has said she'll walk me home, and she will."

Still Elspeth hesitated. "Mum won't like it," she said.

He shrugged. "We won't tell her then. Now you run. You don't want to be late to school." His eyes were dancing. This whole thing seemed to be his idea of a wonderful game.

Again Elspeth shot Diana a look, and this time the hostility was unmistakable. But if Diana had had any doubts about taking the old man's side, the girl's obvious anger blew them all away.

"It's okay," Diana told her, not sure if she meant to reassure or to annoy. "I don't mind . . . really."

Without replying, Elspeth turned abruptly and stalked along the path toward the village. When she reached the stile, she vaulted it and hit the other side running. Either she was terribly late for school or, once she thought about it, she was relieved to turn her grandfather over to somebody else's care.

Me and my big mouth, Diana found herself thinking as she stood in the middle of the cow pasture, alone with this strange man. Cautiously, remembering every warning she had ever been given about strangers, she looked up.

This stranger had the face of an elf, a rather uncombed elf, but a friendly one. And there was something fragile about him, too, as though his bones might be hollow.

Diana felt herself relaxing. What harm could there possibly be in such an ancient little man? "I'll walk you home now," she said, "but you'll have to show me where you live."

In response, he drew himself up and clicked his heels smartly. "Group Captain George Somers, at your service," he announced, and then to Diana's astonishment, he saluted.

5

THERE WERE a few people on the village streets now, and those they passed greeted Group Captain Somers warmly.

"Morning, George," they said or "Good morning, Mr. Somers," and he stopped each time to introduce Diana.

"This pretty lady is Diana Baldwin from Minnesota," he told them, as though both she and being from Minnesota were very special indeed.

Finally he stopped in front of another of the old stone houses, a winding block up from the one where Diana and her mother were staying. "Here it is," he said with a sigh. "This is where my daughter lives." He didn't seem the least bit pleased to have arrived there.

"Oh." Diana searched for something else to say. She was going to be sorry to see him go. Despite what she had told her mother about being perfectly all right alone, the day stretched ahead of her like a desert. She had her letter to write to Lady Di, of course, but she couldn't mail it. She didn't yet know how much postage it would need . . . nor did she have money to buy stamps. And despite what she had told her mother, she didn't feel like reading or watching television.

"Well . . ." The Group Captain seemed as reluctant to separate as she was. He raked his fingers through his bushy hair, leaving it more disarrayed than it had been before. "One walk in the morning. That's all she allows me these days." There was something beyond sadness in his voice, a deep resignation that made Diana want to do something to rescue him, though she wasn't quite sure from what . . . or whom.

"Are you talking about your daughter?"

"Right you are. My daughter." He glanced toward the house as he spoke.

Diana wondered if this cruel daughter of his might be watching from behind the heavy drapes. She was indignant. "But you're grown up. How can she tell you what you can and can't do?"

Group Captain Somers shrugged. "When a man gets old, there's naught they can't tell him it seems." He inclined his head toward the house and added in a conspiratorial whisper, "*She* thinks I should be content to sit in front of the telly all day long, watching old war movies."

"I know," Diana said with real feeling. "It's not fair!" Not that she knew what it was like to be expected to watch television. In fact, her mother had rules about how much TV she was allowed to watch, quite strict rules. But she certainly knew what it was like to have somebody telling her what she was supposed to do every minute of her life.

The old man bent closer. "The folks who make those movies, they don't even know what it was like. They weren't there."

Diana nodded sagely, pretending she had always thought the same thing about war movies, though she had never thought anything about them actually. In fact, she couldn't remember that she had ever watched one.

Group Captain Somers glanced again toward the windows of the house, and his whisper deepened. "I served my country in two world wars, you know."

Diana hadn't known, but she nodded again. She was growing uneasy. Any minute the old man's daughter was probably going to come storming out and grab him by the ear, and she didn't want to be there to watch. Most likely the daughter already had the television turned on and waiting . . . her own subtle form of torture.

Apparently the Group Captain was worried, too, because he motioned for Diana to follow and started back along the cobbled street in the direction they had come from. Diana followed, as relieved to leave the house behind as if she were the one in danger of being yanked inside.

Group Captain Somers talked as they walked, his voice growing stronger as they moved farther from the house. He spoke as though Diana were an equal, an adult. "In the Great War, I was infantry. Stood in mud until our feet rotted, we did. In the Second, I flew bombers." When he said the word *bombers*, he straightened his back a little, and his face glowed with pride. Diana wondered if he was preparing to salute again, but he didn't.

"That must have been scary," she said, more because she wanted to say something than because she had any particular opinion about bombers.

Group Captain Somers drew himself even more erect. "There wasn't room for fear in those planes," he barked. But then he dropped his voice again and added, "Three times I was shot down. Over enemy territory. Three times I near perished in the flames."

Diana kept pace beside the Group Captain, observing him with new respect. To be shot down three times . . . and then to have to go back up again! She couldn't imagine how he had been able to do it. She found herself reaching out, maternally, to pat the rough wool of his sleeve.

Group Captain Somers jerked his arm, as though startled by the touch, and stared at her from beneath his bristly eyebrows. It was almost as if he hadn't expected to find her still there. "Won't your mum be fretting about where you've got to?" he asked, his tone entirely changed. Diana could feel herself shrinking back to child size.

Her cheeks flamed. "Of course not. My mom is in Lincoln. She's working." *My mom is always working*, she could have added, but she didn't.

"Stone the crows!" Group Captain Somers stopped walking and studied her as if she had said something astonishing. "She left you here alone? How old are you, child?"

"Twelve." Diana tried to say it with authority, but it came out sounding like an apology instead. Twelve was such a nothing age, not even a teenager yet, and she wouldn't have another birthday until the next May.

Group Captain Somers scowled. "What in heaven's name is she thinking of, your mum? It's against the law. Children less than thirteen aren't to be left without supervision. Not in this country, they're not!"

All morning Diana had been feeling angry with her mother, furious, in fact, but now she felt a sudden surge of protectiveness toward her . . . and indignation for herself. "I wanted to stay here," she replied sharply. "I'm responsible! At home I even baby-sit for other people's kids. I've been doing it for nearly a year."

Group Captain Somers shook his head firmly. "Well, we certainly don't allow such things here!" And then he muttered to himself, "Children taking care of children!" and shook his head more vigorously still.

"I'm fine." Diana took a step back. "Really!" If her mother got into some kind of trouble for letting her stay alone, Diana was sure to have to spend the next year following her around every single place she went.

"No, you're not fine. You're not fine at all. But we'll soon take care of that." The Group Captain had begun walking once more, toward the center of the village this time, and again he motioned Diana to follow.

"As if somebody asked *him* to look out for me," Diana muttered to herself. For an instant she considered turning and running in the opposite direction.

The old man would never catch her. But then that idea seemed ridiculous. What was there to run from? So she caught up to him and inquired, instead, "What are you going to do?"

"I'll just have to look after you for the day, that's all." Group Captain Somers spoke gruffly, and his mouth was set in a determined line. But when he looked down at Diana, his eyes beneath their fierce brows were smiling.

"Oh." Diana was relieved that he wasn't thinking of doing anything more serious, but she felt rather cautious still. In the first place, she certainly didn't need anybody bossing her around. She got enough of that from her mother.

But then he said, "There's little enough to do here. Perhaps we'll have to take a bit of a ride on the bus, see the sights in Lincoln."

"Oh, I don't think —" she started to say. If her mother had objected to Diana's letting the punker help the day before, what would she say to her going off to Lincoln with a strange old man?

But Group Captain Somers had turned the corner. He was heading up the narrow, main street of Coleby — High Street, it was called — toward the highway and the bus stop. And he went on talking, apparently not even hearing the objections she had begun. "I do believe Lincoln Castle is the place to begin. It would be an educational sight for a child from the States."

"You mean there's a castle, a real live castle in Lincoln?" Diana's mother hadn't mentioned any castle, which just went to show how little attention her mother paid to what was important to her.

Group Captain Somers chuckled. "I don't know about live, but it certainly is real."

Diana hesitated. She knew she should stay here in Coleby. Her mother's rules had always been very firm about what she could do when she was left alone. She wasn't even allowed to baby-sit except when Mom was home so she would be nearby if there was an emergency.

But after all, seeing a castle was one of the things she had dreamed about all her life, and her mother hadn't offered to take her to one, had she? And Group Captain Somers was certainly harmless enough. It wasn't like going somewhere with a stranger the way people warned you about all the time. She could probably blow him over with a good puff of air if he tried to do anything funny.

"What about your daughter?" she asked. "What will she say?"

Group Captain Somers snorted. "Same as she always says, I suspect. Entirely too much. Some folks can't be happy unless they have something to fret about."

"And when will we get back? It'll be before five-thirty, won't it?"

"Of course. We'll be back long before five-thirty." He seemed to be reading Diana's mind. "Is that when your mum gets home, then?"

Diana nodded.

"Good. Then I can meet her. I'll offer my services as

a . . ." For an instant Diana was afraid he was going to say *baby-sitter* or *nanny* or whatever such things were called here, but instead he finished with "companion." Diana loved him instantly for the choice. "I can see you're a good girl," he added, "just like my granddaughter."

Diana thought of the sour, unapproachable girl she had met on the path and wasn't too pleased with the comparison, but still she said, "Thank you, Group Captain Somers!" She skipped a few steps on ahead before stopping and waiting for him to catch up with her again. It would be fun, if only for a day, to pretend that this nice old man was *her* grandpa.

"I've never seen a real castle," she added.

Captain Somers bowed deeply. "Well, then, I'm at your service, Your Ladyship." And he held out his arm the way men did for ladies in the olden days.

Diana knew exactly what to do. She put her hand in the crook of her companion's elbow and fell into step beside him.

It wouldn't be Buckingham Palace, but a castle, any castle, had to be better than staying by herself in Coleby. And if nothing else, she could begin her time in England by proving to her mother that she had better things to do with her life than sitting around waiting for her to come home.

*

Lincoln Castle wasn't at all what Diana had expected. There were no velvet drapes or Persian carpets or crystal chandeliers. In fact, as the Group Captain explained, the old castle had been a fortress and a prison, not a place where people lived . . . especially not a place where royalty would want to live. On the roof at one point there were even iron fittings left from the gallows where criminals had been hung, and one of the towers held a graveyard where prisoners were buried. Diana shivered, though it was a rather delicious shiver.

The old prison chapel was filled with narrow, wooden stalls, each designed to hold a single inmate, standing at attention. The prisoners had been able to see the preacher, but they couldn't have seen any of their fellow inmates. Diana closed first the Group Captain and then herself into separate stalls. What would it be like, she wondered, to be locked in that way and then preached at? It might even be worse than being a kid.

But as she followed the Group Captain down the steps that led back to the courtyard, Diana began to grow uneasy. The castle was interesting, but had it been worth the risk of getting into trouble for coming to Lincoln without permission?

"Would Your Ladyship like a grand tour of the cathedral next?" Group Captain Somers asked, bowing as though she were, indeed, nobility and he was in her service. "The Lincoln imp awaits you there."

"Who's the Lincoln imp?" Diana asked, her curiosity diminished by a thought that began to seize her. Where was the college from here? What would happen if she ran into her mother in town? What could she possibly say? *I changed my mind and decided to come to Lincoln after all . . . with this old man I just met?*

"The Lincoln imp is a devil. He flew into the cathedral when they were building it and got himself turned to stone."

Diana sighed. Did he expect her to believe such stories? Besides, she was starting to feel tired, as if she might have been better off spending the day sleeping. Probably this was the jet lag she had heard people talk about . . . or maybe it was the effect England was going to have on her for the whole time.

"I don't think so," she said. "I'm not much interested in devils."

Group Captain Somers stopped walking and studied her. "What are you interested in, then?" His head cocked to one side at a listening angle, he waited for her answer. He seemed actually to care about what she would say.

"Buckingham Palace." Diana breathed the name as though it were a single word. "I want to go to Buckingham Palace." She stood perfectly still, waiting for Group Captain Somers to laugh at her. Or at least to shrug off what she wanted and go back to talking about the cathedral and its imp.

But he didn't. He stood perfectly still, studying her face intently. "Really?" he said. "That's where you're wanting to go?"

"More than any place in the world," she said . . . *except home*, she could have added, but she didn't.

For a moment he stood there, erect and quiet, and his eyes took on an inward-searching look. "Buckingham Palace," he repeated softly. "Buckingham Palace. Buckingham Palace." And each time he said it, his face grew more lively.

Finally he focused on Diana again. "Then Buckingham Palace it is, Your Ladyship. I have a bit of business there myself." And he turned and headed out of the castle at a pace so rapid that Diana found herself trotting to catch up.

She was breathless. The last thing in the world she had expected was to be taken seriously.

"But Buckingham Palace is in London. That's over a hundred miles away." She felt as if she were explaining something to a child. What was wrong with the Group Captain anyway?

"Of course it is," he replied without slowing his pace.

"Then where are we going?" For the first time it dawned on her that she was completely dependent on this old man and on whatever he decided to do. She hadn't even the few coins of British money it would take to buy a return bus ticket to Coleby from Lincoln. It hadn't occurred to her mother that she would need money yet . . . alone at the cottage in Coleby as she was supposed to be.

"The train station," he replied.

"But the train to London takes almost two hours . . . and two hours back again," she added. She had been on it the day before. She knew.

"Of course. But we've got lots of time. We'll see the Queen and be home in time for tea."

"Time for tea?"

"Supper is what you call it, I think."

"But it's not — " Diana started to object. *It's not the Queen I want to see.*

But she didn't finish. What difference did it make? If they got to Buckingham Palace, if they actually did see the Queen, could Lady Di be far away?

6

GROUP CAPTAIN SOMERS stopped in the open doorway of the Lincoln train station. "Shhhh!" he whispered, raising a gnarled finger to his lips. "They'll hear us!"

"Who?" Diana whispered back, looking around. "There's nobody here."

There was, indeed, no one to be seen but the ticket agent behind the window, and he had his back turned to them.

The Group Captain didn't answer. Instead, he motioned Diana to follow and moved with a quick, shuffling tiptoe through the station to the train platform beyond. Once on the platform, he put the doorway far behind him before lowering himself stiffly onto a concrete bench.

"There," he said, "that's done," as though they had accomplished the most important part of their journey. Still his eyes continued to dart apprehensively in every direction.

Diana sat gingerly on the other end of the bench. She found herself looking around nervously, too, though she didn't know what it was she should be watching for.

"There's a problem about getting to London," the Group Captain said finally, his gaze settling on Diana.

They weren't going to go, after all! Diana couldn't decide whether the knot unraveling in her chest was disappointment or relief. "What's the problem?" she asked.

"The man in there." The Group Captain indicated the station behind them with a slight movement of his head. "The one selling tickets? He's a spy."

"A spy?" Diana looked at Group Captain Somers doubtfully.

He nodded. "For my daughter. She's got them all over town . . . to keep me from doing things, going places. Especially she wants to keep me from going to London and collecting the medal that's waiting for me there."

"What kind of a medal?" Diana felt cautious.

"For valor. In wartime, you see. They're holding it for me. It's the Victoria Cross, and no one can give it but a member of the royal family."

"And your daughter won't let you go to London to receive the Victoria Cross?" Indignation took over where the caution had been. This daughter, Elspeth's mother no doubt, must be some kind of monster. "Why?"

Group Captain Somers shrugged, a small gesture which said that his daughter's cruel whims were quite beyond his comprehension, that he was an old man with no one on his side. His eyes seemed to focus on something far down the tracks.

For a father to be held prisoner by his own daughter! It was terrible! If only there were something she could do to help.

Diana turned to gaze down the tracks, too, but there was nothing to be seen. Nothing worth looking at anyway.

She sat up straighter, the solution suddenly clear. "I know what we'll do. That ticket agent, the one who's a spy? He doesn't know me. You give me the money, and I'll go in and buy tickets for us both."

Group Captain Somers' woeful expression vanished immediately. In fact, he beamed. "What a bright lass you are! Now, who would have thought of such a thing?"

Diana's cheeks warmed with pleasure.

He rummaged in an inner jacket pocket until he produced a wallet. "It's lucky I got my old-age pension yesterday," he said. "Even luckier my daughter hasn't had her bite yet."

There ought to be a law against daughters like that, Diana said to herself as she took the bill he held toward her.

The bill was larger and more papery feeling than American money and strangely colored, almost pink. In fact, Diana noted, English money seemed rather like oversized Monopoly money. She started toward the station.

When she was a few feet away, Group Captain Somers called after her, "Be sure to buy two returns." And then he added, his voice high with excitement, "It's a right fine idea you had there, Sarah."

50 ·

The name caught Diana like a pebble tossed at her back. She stopped and turned to face Group Captain Somers. "What did you say?" she asked.

He seemed to stiffen. "Why, I said, 'It's a right fine idea you had there, Diana.' What did you suppose?"

Diana hesitated for a moment, studying him, but then she turned to her task again. A wrong name wasn't important, was it? And the weight which had taken up residence in her stomach didn't mean anything either. Her stomach was often like that, giving her warnings that she didn't need.

They were going to Buckingham Palace, exactly as she had dreamed. Nothing else mattered.

*

Diana took a seat next to the window of the open coach, facing in the direction they would be moving, and Group Captain Somers sat down opposite her. There was a table between them, and he ran his hands over it repeatedly as if even its ordinary surface were a source of great satisfaction to him. Despite his mane of white hair and his deeply creased skin, he reminded Diana of an excited child.

She watched him with some amusement. Having spent hours on trains the day before, she felt like a seasoned traveler herself.

The sky was still a dull gray, but as the train pulled out of Lincoln, Diana found herself admiring the lush, green landscape. It was accented here and there with fields of a solid, brilliant yellow which her mother had told her the day before was a crop called "rape." Whatever it was called, she had never seen anything so intensely yellow. Its beauty, combined with the thrill of her destination, was almost enough to overcome the tiredness she had been feeling earlier.

What would the kids say when she told them she was friends with Lady Di? For that matter, what would her mother say when Diana told her that she had been to visit a real princess? But then maybe she wouldn't tell her mother at all. Maybe she and Lady Di would keep their friendship a secret.

The thought of her mother, however, was accompanied by a wash of guilt, and Diana's mood took a sudden plunge. Mom would be beside herself if she knew Diana was going off with a stranger this way. And apart from Group Captain Somers' being a stranger — however harmless he might be — Diana's worse crime was going anywhere at all without letting her mother know. It was a firm rule and a courtesy practiced between them without exception: her mother always let Diana know where she would be, and Diana did the same. If Diana and the Group Captain were delayed getting back, or if her mother returned to Coleby early and found her gone . . .

"It's near half a century I've been waiting to receive this medal," Group Captain Somers said, breaking into Diana's reverie.

"Why did it take so long?" she asked, letting her indignation over the Captain's situation replace her concern about her mother.

"Well," he settled into his seat like one preparing to begin a long story, "when the last war was over, times were hard. My daughter was only a little 'un, and then the wife came sick. She had gallbladder, you see. I sent her to hospital many times, but the doctors never did get her right."

He leaned his elbows on the table, forming his hands into a steeple, and went on talking . . . about his wife's health, about her inability to have another child after their daughter was born, about the work he took in Lincoln as an auto mechanic after the Second World War. Diana leaned back against her own seat, letting the talk flow over her. She wondered if he would ever get around to answering the question she had asked.

A man appeared, selling tea and sandwiches from a cart, and though Diana's stomach rumbled loudly, the Group Captain didn't interrupt his monologue to take notice of the passing food. She watched sadly as the cart disappeared into the next car. Enough time had passed that the orange-yolked eggs she had barely touched that morning would have seemed a treat.

Group Captain Somers switched to war stories next. He spoke of Huns and Messerschmitts, of the One-Thousand Plan and the Lancaster bomber. Diana turned her thoughts to her meeting with Lady Di.

She knew she had been foolish to have thought, even briefly, that Lady Di would be able to send her home. Everybody said royalty had little real power these days. But it would be good to meet her, even so. If nothing else, she might give Diana a gift, some kind of memento of their meeting. A picture autographed "To my dear friend, Diana" or something like that.

Then when she did get back home, she could put it up inside her locker door at school.

Oh that, she would say when her friends asked, *that's Lady Di. Princess Diana to you, of course.*

All her classmates would be starting junior high in the fall. It was one of the things that had made coming here so hard. When Diana got back she would be the only one who wouldn't know her way around the big school. Except for the new seventh graders, and she wouldn't want to be associated with *them!* There would have been parties she hadn't attended, too, and jokes she hadn't shared. She would be on the outside again.

Just think how impressed they'll be that you've been living overseas, her mother had said. *You can tell them all about England.* But Diana knew better than that. It was the kind of thing her mother always said, and Diana might have been naive enough to believe it when she was a little kid. Teachers would be impressed, all right, probably impressed enough to ask embarrassing questions in front of the class. But somebody living other places wasn't the kind of thing kids got excited about.

If she could bring something home from Lady Di, though, some proof that she had actually met her, that they had gotten to know one another, the kids would notice that.

"Traveling again, I see, Group Captain Somers." It was the conductor, taking tickets, and Diana looked up in surprise.

So the Group Captain was recognized even on the

train. He must be more famous than Diana had thought, not just a veteran, but a real war hero. She sat up straighter and smiled at the conductor, wanting him to notice that she and the Group Captain were together.

But Group Captain Somers seemed to be more flustered by the greeting than pleased. When he took the tickets back, his hands shook slightly, and splotchy patches of pink appeared on his cheeks.

"Taking Sarah, here, down to Buckingham Palace," he mumbled, nodding toward Diana, his eyes averted from the conductor's face.

There it was again. *Sarah.* The name didn't feel like a pebble this time. It felt like something much larger, a boulder maybe. And it sent an intensely uncomfortable question rippling through Diana like waves after the boulder's splash. Did she want to be going off to London with someone who couldn't even remember who she was?

The conductor nodded in a friendly enough way, but he gave Diana a searching look before moving on. It was as if he knew Group Captain Somers had made a mistake about her name. For a brief moment, Diana thought about telling the conductor she had changed her mind and wanted to go back, asking him how she could do it.

But when she turned to look after him, he was already pushing open the door into the next car. Should she run after him? No. She would feel silly doing that. Besides, nothing so terrible had happened, had it? The Group Captain had made a mistake about her name.

That was all. Lots of people mixed up names. Her friend Meghan had three sisters, and Meghan's mother sometimes went through the names of all three sisters, two cats, and the dog before she said Meghan, especially when she was exasperated.

Diana took a deep breath and turned back to her companion, who was looking even more upset than she felt.

He leaned toward her, speaking in a hoarse whisper. "He's one of them. One of her spies." He was wringing his hands as he spoke, his palms making a papery sound as they rubbed together.

More spies? Diana didn't know whether to believe him or not. "It doesn't look like he's going to do anything," she pointed out.

"He'll report me, that's what he'll do. He'll call back to the Lincoln station, and then they'll call *her*." Group Captain Somers was becoming quite agitated.

"Who? Your daughter?" This Sarah he had on his mind so much had to be his daughter. And what could Sarah do to him if she found out anyway?

"That's it. My daughter." Group Captain Somers had half risen from his seat, looking up and down the aisle as if he were expecting his daughter to emerge from the next car. Diana had a vision of an enormous woman with small, mean eyes and a switchblade in one hand.

"But I'm sure Sarah wouldn't —" she started to say only to be startled into silence by a short, sharp bark of laughter.

"Who?" the Group Captain asked. "Who did you say?"

Diana's ears grew instantly hot. Obviously she had made a mistake. "Your daughter. I thought her name was Sarah."

The old man shook his head vigorously. "My daughter's name is Dolores," he said, "Dolores Graham. She married Timothy Graham, you see." And he was off talking again, his concern about the conductor and the very name Sarah apparently forgotten.

Diana leaned back slowly in her seat. She had quit trying to listen. Clearly Group Captain Somers was a bit . . . well, funny. And here she was on her way to London with him. How could she have been so dumb?

She had no money. This was a strange country where she didn't know her way around. And if Group Captain Somers lost his grip altogether, she wouldn't begin to know what to do.

She couldn't just ask the nearest adult for help, because if she did that, she was sure to get her mother into trouble for leaving her alone to start with. Maybe more trouble than she had dreamed. Hadn't Group Captain Somers said it was against the law in England for kids her age to be left alone?

She had been lucky yesterday, finding the punker, and she had been lucky then because her mother had known where to look . . . and because nobody could be blamed. Not her mother. Not her. Getting separated on the underground had been an accident. That was all. But being on this train with Group Captain Somers was no accident, and she had a feeling she wasn't going to be able to count on luck today.

Maybe she couldn't even count on the kind of luck it was going to take to get in to see Lady Di. Maybe her mother had been right, after all, and the Princess didn't see visitors, not old men wanting medals, not girls wanting . . .

What was it that she had wanted? To meet Lady Di. To have Lady Di see her. That was all. That wasn't too much to ask, was it?

The man in customs and the punker had both said . . . What had they said exactly? That Lady Di would be "proud to meet an American lass with such a fine name." That she knew "about girls' dreams."

They weren't just jollying her along, were they? Condescending to her, the way people sometimes did with kids?

No. They couldn't have been. Diana could smell that kind of thing a mile away.

Then why did she feel as though she was waking from a dream, the kind of dream that slipped away before she could quite recall what it had been?

Diana leaned her head back against the seat and turned it gently from side to side. It was what her mother always did when she had been working over her books or her typewriter too long and her neck was stiff. The train wheels made a steady, clacking rhythm that seemed to originate inside her brain.

Diana Baldwin, they sang. *Diana Baldwin. You're in trouble . . . trouble . . . trouble . . . trouble . . . trouble . . .*

7

DIANA STEPPED down off the train into the echoing cavern of Kings Cross Station. The Group Captain had descended just in front of her, and she took hold of his sleeve and pulled him to a stop beside her.

"Yes?" he said, looking down at her warily, his eyebrows raised like two bushy flags.

"Captain Somers," she said, struggling against the tremor that was trying to invade her voice, "I have an idea."

"Group Captain," he corrected, almost sternly.

"Group Captain," Diana repeated, annoyed at the correction. What was a Group Captain anyway? One of a whole group of people who got made captain? It didn't sound very special to her. "I think we should go back. On the next train, I mean. My mother's going to be awfully worried . . . and your daughter, Doris."

"Dolores," he corrected again, more gently this time, but then he grinned and added. "Dolores is always worried. It's her main satisfaction in life . . . fretting about her poor old dad."

"But —" Diana started to say.

He interrupted. "Besides I haven't come all this way to go home again without my medal. It's my due!"

Diana realized guiltily that she had almost forgotten part of the reason for their coming here was for the Group Captain to get his Victoria Cross. It *was* his due, after all, and it was quite disgraceful that he had been made to wait so long. She only wished she was still so certain that barging in on the royal family was *her* due as well.

How had she managed to convince herself that Lady Di would want to meet her, anyway? Just because they shared a name? There must be hundreds of other Dianas right here in England. Thousands, maybe.

Group Captain Somers started walking, and she followed, feeling a bit lightheaded.

A clock loomed on the station wall ahead of them. It was after one already. There was no way they could locate Lady Di and be back in Coleby before her mother returned at five-thirty. Even if everything went smoothly and they got back just under the wire, the buses to Coleby ran only once an hour. They would end up on the same bus from Lincoln with her mother. And wouldn't that require some fancy explanations?

Maybe she could say that she had seen that Group Captain Somers needed help, so she had gone with him.

All the way to London?

Maybe she would say that if her mother was so concerned about her, she ought to try staying home once in a while to take care of her, to keep her out of trouble. All Diana's life her mother had been leaving her alone, running off to one job or another. Well, not leaving her alone exactly. At least not until recently when Mom had begun to agree she was old enough to stay by herself. But leaving her with a baby-sitter or in a day-care center, which was almost as bad.

Wasn't it a mother's job to stay around long enough to teach her daughter responsibility?

Diana tried to imagine herself blaming her mother for her own lack of responsibility, and the very thought made her wince. Responsibility was one of her mother's major themes. She would never buy the idea that she was to blame for Diana's failure to be responsible.

It might be worth trying another tack with the Group Captain, though. She tugged on his sleeve again. "Look at us," she said, gesturing first to her own sweatshirt and jeans and then to his worn tweed jacket and baggy trousers. "We're not exactly dressed to visit royalty, are we?"

But as she had already half expected, he didn't even pause to glance at his clothes or hers. Instead, he replied, "Clothes don't make the man . . . or the girl, either."

Diana sighed loudly, but of course that didn't faze him at all. Maybe she was the only person in the world who was bothered by sighing.

"Why don't you just give me my ticket then," she suggested finally, though it was the least attractive solution of all. "I'll go back to Lincoln by myself. Maybe my mother will bring me to Buckingham Palace another time."

Group Captain Somers paused, just briefly, and for an instant Diana thought she might have said the right thing at last. But then he began shaking his head vigorously. "Take a train back alone? What can you be thinking of, girl?" And he began walking again toward a sign which said UNDERGROUND.

Diana stood where she was, watching the old man walk away. She wanted to stomp her feet and scream, but she doubted that Group Captain Somers would pay any more attention to that than he did to her arguments. Surely though, he would stop when he noticed she wasn't with him.

He didn't, though. In fact, he kept moving at a determined pace that seemed to increase in vigor as the distance between them grew. And he didn't once look back. Diana had a sudden sick feeling that *he* was escaping from *her,* and she found herself running to catch up. She had never felt more frustrated . . . or more alone.

If only she had the number with her that Mom had left by the phone in Coleby. She could call and ask her mother for help. Mom would be furious, but she would have to do something. As it was, though, Diana not only didn't have the number with her but she couldn't even remember the name of the college where her mother was working. It was something strange. Saint Gross? No. She should have paid more attention.

Whatever else happened, she had to stay with the old man. He might be a bit strange, but he had her return ticket to Lincoln . . . and bus money for when they got there. She couldn't help beginning to wonder, though, if his dream of seeing a member of the royal family was as foolish as hers had been. Even if he did have an important medal coming.

Anybody who knew anything about the royal family knew they didn't spend their time rushing out to meet visitors. That was what her mother had said. And somebody who had lived in England all his life should know it even better than she did!

Diana's mother had been right to criticize her about dreaming all the time. She was never going to dream again . . . in her entire life.

Not even at night when she went to bed.

*

"That's Buckingham Palace?"

Diana stared, unbelieving, across the swirling traffic at the large, gray building. It sprawled over a wide area, but it wasn't particularly tall. It certainly wasn't beautiful, and it seemed to be constructed of the same gray stone everything else in England was made of. Besides all that, it was surrounded by a high iron fence. There was no way to get near the palace itself . . . or even near any of the guards, for that matter.

"Right you are; that's Buckingham Palace." Group Captain Somers spoke with unmistakable pride, and then, apparently sensing Diana's disappointment, he added, "Of course, there's more to see when they're changing the guard. That's what folks come for mostly."

Diana looked first to her left, then to her right at the cars, taxis, and red, double-decker buses that seemed to charge out of nowhere and off again without ever slowing their frantic pace. The road in front of the palace circled a memorial (to Queen Victoria, the Group Captain had explained), and the traffic scurried around it unceasingly. It was as if a fountain and a group of statues were an entirely unremarkable obstruction in a road, and a palace, however unimpressive, just a common sight to be driving past.

The day seemed to be growing cooler instead of warmer, and Diana shivered and wrapped her arms around herself. "Lady Di probably isn't home right now, anyway," she said.

"Lady Di?" Group Captain Somers stopped studying the traffic as if it were some kind of battle plan and stared at her. "It's Lady Di you're looking to see?"

"Of course," Diana snapped. "I told you that in the beginning."

The moment she had said it — *I told you* — she knew she was wrong. She hadn't told him. She had said only that she wanted to see Buckingham Palace. And that was where he had insisted on bringing her, even after she had changed her mind about wanting to come.

"Aren't Lady Di and Prince Charles at Buckingham Palace?" she asked, more humbly now, almost in a tone of apology. But she already knew the answer from the expression on the Group Captain's face.

"No, they're at Kensington Palace. That's a bit of a distance from here."

Diana clenched her teeth and turned away. This was too much. Everything had gone wrong since she had arrived in this stupid country. Everything. First she had gotten lost on the underground; then her mom had gone off to work her first full day there; then she had met that hateful girl, and she had allowed herself to be carried off to London by this old man who called her other people's names. And now on top of it all, Buckingham Palace was ugly and Lady Di didn't even live there.

Diana was afraid she was about to sit down, right there in the middle of the sidewalk, and bawl like a little kid.

"Your Ladyship, I have an idea." Group Captain Somers was bending over her, his face furrowed with concern, his voice cajoling.

Diana rammed her fists into her jeans pockets and looked off in the other direction. "What?" she asked, in a tone which made it perfectly clear that whatever his idea was it wouldn't do any good. Nothing he came up with would make any difference anyway . . . unless he could figure out some way to send her and her mother back to Minnesota. At this point, she would have settled for going back by herself without her mother.

She could move in with Meghan, the way they had both talked about so many times. Or if Meghan's mother wouldn't agree to that, she could go live in her own house. There were people leasing it, but they didn't have any kids. Why should they care if she moved back into her own room?

"We'll get us a copy of *The Daily Telegraph*!" Group Captain Somers announced, triumphantly.

Diana stared at him. As if all their problems would be solved by the simple act of buying a newspaper! But he went right on beaming at her, clearly delighted with his idea.

"That'll do a lot of good," she said.

She had meant her words to be sarcastic, but Group Captain Somers apparently missed the sarcasm entirely. He nodded vigorously. "It will. You'll see. We'll find Lady Di. And I can get my medal from her as well as any of them."

Saying this, he turned back and set off at a shuffling trot toward the large, open park they had already walked through on their approach to Buckingham Palace.

Diana followed, her own steps dragging. It didn't seem to make much difference where she went, anyway. They obviously weren't going back to Lincoln until Group Captain Somers was good and ready.

A moment before, faced with the bustling traffic, the Group Captain had seemed uncertain and old. Now he was all confidence again, and he held his head high. Unfortunately, his confidence did nothing to reassure Diana.

On the other side of the park, he entered a shop that sold periodicals, stationery supplies, and candy. Diana followed. While he picked out his newspaper, she stopped before a glass counter filled with candy. Just looking at the display made the saliva rush to her mouth.

"Do you want a sweetie, duck?" the woman behind the counter asked, and though Diana's stomach growled its own response, she shook her head. She could ask Group Captain Somers for money, she supposed, but somehow she didn't want to do that. She wasn't sure how much he got for his old-age pension, anyway, even before his daughter's "bite." Maybe he didn't buy food because he didn't have enough money left or he was afraid of returning to his daughter with all of it spent.

Besides, he was riffling through a newspaper and didn't seem any more aware of the candy than he had been of the cart of sandwiches on the train. *That must be why he's so shriveled up,* Diana decided, *because he forgets to eat.*

"Here it is," he said at last, practically dancing over to Diana's side. And then he added, beaming at her over the top of the paper, "We're in luck."

Diana didn't ask what he meant. It was, she thought, a bit late for luck to start operating now. He didn't wait for her to ask, however. He held the open paper in front of her and pointed to something in the middle of the page titled "Court Circular."

"Well?" she asked, glancing at it without reading beyond the column head.

He stabbed the paper with a thickened finger. "This tells about the appearances of all the members of the royal family." And now he was reading aloud. "'The Princess of Wales this afternoon attends a garden party at the Queen Mary Gardens in Regent's Park.'"

He looked back at Diana, beaming, and when she didn't respond, he explained, "The Princess of Wales is Lady Di. That's who you want to see, right?"

"Oh. Right." Diana's head was spinning. But she didn't want to see Lady Di anymore, did she? Lady Di wasn't going to be able to do anything for her. And besides, Diana wasn't going to let herself get caught up in dreaming again. She had decided. Hadn't she?

"It's a tea for the Save the Children fund," Group Captain Somers said.

Diana nodded, mute.

"And you're a child, after all." The Group Captain was smiling broadly.

A child who needed saving? Diana took the paper and inspected the notice herself. That was, indeed, what it said. *The Princess of Wales. Queen Mary Gardens. Save the Children.*

Clearly her mother was wrong. Here it was in black and white. Lady Di was going to be in a public park where anyone, even old men and twelve-year-old girls, could simply walk up and speak to her.

She folded the newspaper and handed it back to Group Captain Somers. Then she took a deep breath, letting hope flow back into her lungs with the air.

"I'm ready," she said.

8

ON THE UNDERGROUND to Regent's Park, Diana let herself slip the rest of the way into the spell of the Group Captain's enthusiasm. She was here, wasn't she? She might as well make good use of the trip.

She even began to compose the speech she was going to deliver to Lady Di.

"I'm a half-orphan," she would say. "My mother has stolen me away from everything I ever loved. My father" — surely she had loved him once, hadn't she? —"my home, my friends."

No. That wasn't the way to begin. Maybe she wouldn't have to say anything. Maybe Lady Di would simply look at her and see what she needed, without her having to explain. This woman who was loved by everybody in the entire world would look at her and know.

That she was afraid sometimes. That sometimes she felt entirely alone. That occasionally she would awaken in the middle of the night certain that her mother was going to leave her, too, the way she had left her father. That as long as Diana could remember she had known there was some secret, something dangerous her mother wasn't telling her, and whatever it was lay there between them like a hidden mine, waiting to blow everything up.

Lady Di's parents were divorced, too. Maybe that was one of the reasons Diana wanted so much to meet her. She would understand it all, almost without a word passing between them.

Diana was certain of it.

*

Diana and Group Captain Somers emerged from the underground into a fine mist that deepened the chill without seeming to make anything really wet.

"It's raining," Diana wailed. "They've probably canceled the whole thing!"

The old man inspected the sky as though it were one of the things under the authority of a Group Captain. "'Tisn't raining," he announced. "It's only spitting." He winked at Diana. "Besides, if they shut things down around here for a bit of rain, all of England would be canceled by now."

Diana smiled hopefully and brushed the dewy moisture from her face. He was undoubtedly right. A bit of rain wouldn't stop an English princess any more than it could stop her, Diana Baldwin from Minnesota.

And if everything had been against them at Buckingham Palace, it was *for* them now. There was a traffic light to make crossing the street into the park easy, and once they were in Regent's Park there were signs directing them to the Queen Mary Gardens. Their luck had changed.

Group Captain Somers moved confidently, and soon they could see a profusion of flowers and a crowd gathered that seemed from a distance almost like more and larger flowers. The women, Diana saw as they approached, were wearing pastel dresses and matching hats and some were holding colorful umbrellas as well. The men, unbelievably, were in cutaway coats with tails.

Diana, once more, looked at her clothes and at the Group Captain's. They were both getting more bedraggled-looking by the minute — the fine rain did penetrate when given enough time — and they could hardly have been more out of place if they had come in their pajamas.

There were a great many people at the party, and a large number of police as well, bobbies with their uncomfortable-looking chin straps and with nightsticks attached to their belts. The bobbies made Diana uneasy, but not nearly as uneasy as she felt when she saw that the entire affair was surrounded by wooden barricades. They were set up all around the area and patrolled diligently. Was it possible that she and the Group Captain had come all this distance only to be turned away without so much as a glimpse of Lady Di?

But Group Captain Somers didn't seem to be troubled by the barriers. In fact, he moved along them with a casual confidence that made the outskirts of a royal party seem the most natural place in the world for a rain-soaked old man to be taking a stroll. And then, to Diana's astonishment, just after passing one of the patrolling bobbies, he stooped and crawled clumsily but rapidly beneath the barricade. Emerging on the other side, he scrambled to his feet and disappeared into the crowd.

Diana hesitated for just a fraction of a second before scampering after him. She wondered, though, as she ducked beneath the wooden barrier herself, if crashing a royal party might be reason enough for being arrested in England. She remembered all too well the gallows and the prisoners' chapel stalls at the castle in Lincoln.

As Diana pushed through the crowd, she caught a glimpse of the Group Captain, who had already made good headway toward the center of the gathering. She tried to follow, but a clump of women stood directly in her path, and she had to wend her way around them. They were balancing tea cups on small plates filled with food and eating as steadily as they were talking. One of the women looked down at Diana and scowled, clearly offended by her presence.

Diana sniffed. Save the Children, indeed! These people couldn't even recognize a hungry child in their midst!

But when she had finally reached the point where she thought she had seen the Group Captain last, he was gone. Before her, however, was a large, colorful canopy and tables spread with every kind of cake and cookie she had ever imagined. *Biscuits*, she reminded herself, looking at them hungrily. Her mother had told her that cookies were called "biscuits" here. But whatever they were called, they looked delicious.

Diana glanced around. She couldn't see the Group Captain anywhere, and she couldn't see Lady Di either. Though occasionally someone looked at her with curiosity or disapproval, most of the people seemed to pay no attention to her at all. It was one of those times when there was an advantage in being a child and invisible to the adult world.

The food drew her. Plates of it, stacks of it. Minuscule sandwiches in all shapes, and colorful squares of cake, frosted on every side. There was even a swan carved in ice that seemed to be floating in a huge bowl of strawberry-colored punch. Diana reached out to touch the table, and to her own surprise, her hand came away cupping a red satin rosette.

She looked down at the skillfully shaped ribbon. She hadn't really meant to take it, but at least it was something connected with Lady Di. Something she could take to school when she finally got home. She could tell all her friends that it came from the party she had attended with the Princess of Wales. Maybe she could even say that the Princess herself had presented it.

Diana turned the rosette over. The pin that had held it to the table was still attached. She should put it back. She had been foolish to take it. No one at home would ever believe this little ribbon had anything to do with Lady Di, anyway. It could have come from anywhere.

If she was going to steal, at least she should have been smart enough to take something to eat. That would have made sense. Still, scanning the crowd guiltily, Diana stuffed the rosette, straight pin and all, into her pocket.

And then she saw her. Lady Di! Diana would have recognized her anywhere. The almost shyly lowered chin, the pretty face and slender frame, the beautiful clothes. The Princess was wearing a pale blue suit and a hat made of some kind of matching fabric that seemed to give off its own light. She stood on the other side of the food tables, beneath the canopy, looking extremely royal . . . and incredibly young!

But young or not, here she was, and Diana didn't need the Group Captain any longer. She didn't need anyone. She started around the tables, a thousand questions spinning in her brain. How did a person address a princess? Your Royal Highness? And did she dare simply walk up to Lady Di and start talking, or were you supposed to be introduced?

But even as the questions spun, unanswered, she already knew what she would do. In lots of the pictures she'd seen of Lady Di some child was presenting her with flowers. And despite all the flowers already growing in the garden, vases and vases of cut floral arrangements had been brought in for the party. This would be easy.

Diana snatched up a large bunch of flowers from an ugly, copper vase. The bouquet was too unwieldy for her to manage gracefully, but she crushed it against her chest — there was something in it that gave off an unpleasantly dusty smell — and moved forward with trembling determination.

Lady Di was talking to a woman with stiff, lilac-colored hair. Or, rather, she was listening instead of talking, her attention completely concentrated on the woman's face. Diana, who had always been taught not to interrupt adult conversations, let alone the conversation of a princess, found herself immobilized at Lady Di's side.

Out of the corner of her eye, she could see a bobby moving in her direction. Was he headed for her? Clearly, she hadn't time left to worry about being polite.

But even as she stepped in front of Lady Di with the bobby no more than ten feet away, she realized that she still had no idea how to begin.

"Your Majesty," she tried, "I . . . uh . . . I . . . ." Her chest felt tight and her voice came out sounding high and breathy. "I'd like to present this bouquet. It's from all the children in Minneapolis," and she held out the clumsy tangle of flowers.

Lady Di looked bewildered, so Diana added, "That's in Minnesota . . . in the middle of the United States, you know. Near Canada? But we really do have summer there. Better than yours, actually."

She hadn't meant to say any of that. It just seemed to be on her tongue, waiting to pop out.

Lady Di was glancing around, almost as though she were expecting some kind of rescue.

"And also," Diana said quickly, "there's an old man here. Group Captain George Somers. He wants —"

Two bobbies, one of whom Diana hadn't even noticed before, closed in on her, one on each side.

"It's all right, ma'am, we'll take care of this," one of them said, and Diana found herself propelled backward, her feet lifted off the ground.

"Wait," she called, dropping the flowers and trying to shake herself free, "I've got to talk to Lady Di!"

She could see Lady Di watching her, but then more bobbies appeared, and the Princess, too, was being led away . . . in the opposite direction.

"Stop!" Diana shouted. "Please, stop!" However, no one seemed to hear her at all, least of all the men who had hold of her arms.

9

THE MEN RELEASED Diana finally on the other side of the wooden barrier, directly in front of Group Captain Somers, who also seemed to be under the supervision of a pair of bobbies. A man wearing an old-fashioned tuxedo and a high silk hat was there as well. He appeared to be in charge, so Diana assumed he must be a plainclothesman of some kind.

If she hadn't been so flustered and so angry, the idea of a plainclothesman in a cutaway coat and tails would have been enough to make her smile.

The man in the tuxedo had clearly been trying to interrogate Group Captain Somers, who was glowering stubbornly at the ground.

Diana rubbed her arms — they weren't bruised, actually, but her feelings certainly were — and glared at the bobbies who had dragged her so unceremoniously away from her conversation with Lady Di.

"I must speak to the Princess of Wales," she said, but she sounded, even to herself, like a petulant child. In any case, neither of the bobbies responded. They seemed to be waiting for the plainclothesman to do something.

"This man has come to see her, too," Diana added,

raising her voice a notch. She indicated the Group Captain. "He's going to receive a medal."

"A medal?" inquired the man in the tuxedo. "What kind of a medal would that be, now?"

Diana looked to the Group Captain to explain, but his head simply drooped lower until it protruded from his shoulders like a turtle's from its shell. His mouth was clamped shut.

Diana stepped toward the plainclothesman. "Group Captain Somers is a war hero. He was shot down three times over enemy territory . . . in flames."

The plainclothesman and one of the bobbies exchanged a look, one Diana couldn't decipher, but before either of them could say anything, she continued. "He's come to receive the Victoria Cross, from Lady Di." And then she added, "And I've come to see her, too, because . . ."

She let her sentence trail off, unfinished. There was, after all, nothing about her reasons for coming which could be explained, particularly to the police. Instead, she waited for one of the men to say something or for Group Captain Somers to speak for himself. It was maddening the way he went silent at the most inconvenient moments.

"The Victoria Cross!" one of the bobbies exclaimed at last, and from the group someone let out a snorting laugh.

"This old duffer thinks he's going to get the Victoria Cross?" inquired a young bobby, probably the one who had laughed. His voice was high with amusement. "Gor blimey!"

The man in the tuxedo gave the questioner a withering look, and he fell silent. Diana turned her plea to the young one, anyway. At least he had spoken to her.

"Why not? Why can't Lady Di give him the Victoria Cross? She's a member of the royal family, isn't she? And the Victoria Cross has to be given by a member of the royal family, doesn't it?"

No one answered, not even the young man. In fact, everyone standing in a tight circle around her, including the Group Captain, seemed to have found someplace else to look, if only the ground. Diana glared first at one uncommunicative face then at another, waiting.

Finally the tall man with gray hair spoke. "The Victoria Cross," he explained, "is the highest medal a soldier can receive."

Diana nodded. She understood that.

"It is given in time of war. In fact," he added gently, "that's the *only* time it is given."

She stared at him, uncomprehending. She had heard the words, but they didn't make sense to her. The Second World War had been over for nearly fifty years. "Then why didn't Group Captain Somers get his Victoria Cross while the war was still going on?" she demanded.

Again there was silence, and Diana looked to Group Captain Somers himself for an explanation. His face, however, was a perfect blank, as if none of this had anything to do with him.

Finally the plainclothesman spoke again, choosing his words as though they were valuable coins, each one to be spent with care. "Perhaps he has already received his medal and has simply . . . forgotten. Or maybe" — here he hesitated as if the coins had grown more difficult to select —" he didn't actually earn a Victoria Cross, after all. Very few do, you know."

Diana shook her head emphatically. "But he did. I know. He just hasn't been able to get to London to receive it. First his daughter was too small, then his wife had gallbladder, and then . . ." Several of the bobbies' mouths were twitching in a most annoying manner. It was the kind of look that means the same thing in every country . . . that they found her an amusing child. And though she still couldn't let herself believe what she already knew, that Group Captain Somers didn't have a medal coming, that she had been foolish to believe he did, she quit trying to explain.

"Where do you and Group Captain Somers live?" the plainclothesman asked, breaking the awkward silence.

At first Diana wasn't going to answer, wasn't going to say anything at all to these people. But looking at the man's long, kindly face, she knew he was actually trying to help.

"Coleby," she said finally since the Group Captain still wasn't talking. "He lives in Coleby, near Lincoln." And then she added miserably, "And I guess I do, too."

"How did you and he get here?" the man asked again. Though he was soft spoken, it was clear he was accustomed to receiving answers to all his questions.

"By train." And then Diana went on to explain before he could ask the next question. "We have round-trip tickets. I bought them in Lincoln with his old-age pension."

"You're American, aren't you?" he asked. "Are you visiting in Coleby?"

Diana nodded. That was what it was, after all. A long visit.

"And will you be able to get your grandfather back home?"

Diana looked at the plainclothesman with surprise, less because he thought Group Captain Somers was her grandfather than because he seemed to think she needed to be the one in charge of getting both of them back to Coleby. Still she said, "Of course."

"Then I suggest you head back to the station now before it gets any later. As you see, the party here is over, and the Princess of Wales has already gone back to Kensington Palace."

Diana looked toward the spot where she had met — or nearly met — Lady Di. There was the bouquet of flowers she had presented, lying in a tangled clump, but the people were beginning to drift away. The rain was falling harder, and the Princess of Wales was nowhere in sight. Apparently she hadn't returned after the police had led her away.

Diana's mother had been right about Lady Di. She wasn't really free. After all, the police had seemed as much in charge of her as they had been of Diana. And then, too, Diana wondered if Lady Di really enjoyed talking to lilac-haired ladies at tea parties. Maybe that was simply part of the required training for the next Queen of England. Perhaps she would rather have been home with her children.

Diana turned to Group Captain Somers. "I guess it's time to go back," she said.

But the Group Captain didn't respond. He didn't even seem to hear her. He simply stood there, staring into space, listless and unseeing.

Diana understood now why the plainclothesman had asked if she could get them both back to Lincoln. She also knew that she couldn't. She had no more idea of how to find the train station than she had known the day before how to get back to her mother when she was lost on the underground. And this time there wasn't a friendly punker to tell her what to do. She could hardly ask for help from the police, either. If she told them the whole truth about her situation, she would get her mother into trouble for sure.

"Group Captain Somers," she pleaded, but his eyes didn't even flicker.

She tugged on his sleeve, and still he didn't respond. She could see the concern growing on the plainclothesman's face. She could also see that he was about to start asking another whole series of questions. She had to do something to save herself . . . to save both of them.

She had chosen to go, first to Lincoln, then to London, with this foolish old man, and now it was up to her to get them back as well.

Maybe if she could convince him that his mission had been accomplished.

"Just a moment," she said to the plainclothesman. "Please." She reached into her pocket and extracted the rosette she had taken from the table. Probably they would arrest her for stealing now, but it was the only thing she could think of that might help.

She tugged at the crushed ribbon to pull it back into shape.

"Group Captain George Somers," she said in the most regal voice she could command, "I, Diana, award you the Victoria Cross," and she pinned the satin rosette to the lapel of his ancient, tweed jacket.

Group Captain Somers blinked, looked down at his lapel, and blinked again, his face twisted in what seemed to be pain. Diana held her breath. Had it been a mistake? Not just coming here, but trying to reach the Group Captain this way?

One of the bobbies spoke, the young one. "Tell him what it's for," he said.

Diana nodded, then said the first thing that came to her mind. "It's red for flames, for bravery."

"For valor," the plainclothesman added softly.

Group Captain Somers seemed to be coming back to life. He bent close to Diana and whispered hoarsely in her ear, "Is Sarah here? Is she seeing?"

Diana closed her eyes. Sarah again. What did she have to do with this Sarah? But she whispered back, "Of course she sees," and that seemed to be all Group Captain Somers needed.

He drew himself up into a fine military posture and saluted. Diana was both grateful and amazed when the guards, one by one, came to attention and returned the salute.

Group Captain Somers held his pose, chest out, shoulders back, one hand raised to his rain-dampened forehead. Beneath the salute, tears marked a jagged path down his cheeks.

10

"AND THEN," Group Captain Somers was saying, "another engine started to burn. There were flames coming from our tail, too. I knew my gunner was hit, but I couldn't tell how bad he was."

Diana jerked her head up. She had been falling asleep again. She didn't know which was longer, the train ride from London to Lincoln or the Group Captain's supply of war stories. It was amazing how he had come to life after receiving that bit of red ribbon. He had even thought to buy fish and chips for both of them on their way to the station — a paper cone of crisp fish and french fries with fragrant, dark vinegar poured over all of it — which seemed to revive him even further. It was also amazing that anyone could have been shot down so many times and survived.

If, indeed, he had been shot down all those times.

Diana pushed the thought away. Group Captain Somers might have been confused about having a Victoria Cross coming, but surely his stories of what he had done in the war were true. The plainclothesman was undoubtedly right. Group Captain Somers had already received his Victoria Cross and simply forgotten, the way old people did sometimes. Or if he hadn't received it, he surely should have. Perhaps no one had told the royal family about his war record. There must be lots of men in a war who did brave things without ever getting a medal.

She looked out of the train window, but night had fallen and the window was little more than a blackened mirror reflecting her own face. Her hair looked rumpled, her skin sallow. They definitely had not made it back "in time for tea" . . . or before her mother and the Group Captain's daughter would have realized they were gone. In fact, judging from the clock she had seen in Kings Cross Station, it would be after ten when they finally got back to Lincoln.

She had been right about the trouble she was heading for, that was for sure. In fact, she couldn't even imagine what her mother was going to say or do when they were finally reunited.

The Group Captain went on with his stories, stroking the ribbon in his lapel absently as he spoke. "I was flying a Beaufighter. Carrying bombs. She was a good plane, but nose heavy. If you were shot down over the Channel, you were done."

"Who's Sarah?" Diana asked abruptly. Suddenly she had to know. She had a feeling that once they were back in Coleby, she might not see much of the Group Captain again. She wasn't certain, in fact, that she wanted to see him anymore, but still she wanted things tied up between them before they parted.

He looked up, his face creased into a frown. "Sarah? Who told you about Sarah?"

Diana hesitated. Maybe she shouldn't have asked. "Uh . . . you did. You mentioned her a couple of times. I figured she must be somebody kind of important."

Group Captain Somers didn't reply. He turned to look out the window instead. Or at the window. Diana could see his face reflected back from the impervious black surface of the glass.

"Was Sarah your wife?" she asked gently.

"My wife?" He shook his head. "My wife's name was Gertrude. When you live as long as I have, there's lots who leave you behind." He hesitated, ran his fingers through his unruly hair. "Sarah," he said at last, "Sarah was my baby sister. She died when I was just a lad."

So long ago? Diana mused, and then because she didn't know what else to say, she said, "I'm sorry."

The Group Captain rubbed the window with his sleeve and leaned toward it, as though the darkness were merely a haze on the glass which he could wipe away. When he began to speak again it was in a faraway voice, both more distant and more pain-filled than the one he used in telling his war stories.

"It were a dry summer," he said quietly. "Unusual for Yorkshire. Nobody knew how the pasture caught."

He stopped, and Diana waited for more. When it seemed he wasn't going to offer anything further she prodded him. "What do you mean, caught? Did the pasture catch fire?"

He nodded, but remained silent, staring at the dark- ened landscape. Diana could see the reflection of his face clearly, except for his eyes. The face in the window showed only smudges where his pale blue eyes would be.

"And Sarah was your sister," she prompted once more.

Again he nodded, but still he didn't continue. Just when Diana had decided he would never say more, that she would be left forever with the puzzle of the few fragments he had presented, he began again.

"She had a special spot, near a stone wall, where she fancied playing. When first I saw the fire, I called to her, tried to get her to come away. But she was afeared and she wouldna do. She crouched there by the wall, covering her eyes. Like if she couldna see the flames coming at her, she'd be safe."

He wiped the glass once again with his sleeve, leaned toward it more intently. "I ran for me dad then. He were at the barn, and when I called him out, he went into the fire after her. He tried everything to reach her, he did, but it weren't no use. He just got hisself burned as well. Terrible burned."

Group Captain Somers turned back slowly to face Diana, but he wasn't looking at her. He didn't seem to be looking at anything. "I could hear her cry. I could see the flames dancing all around. But me . . . I didn't have a man's courage. I stood and watched. That's all. Just stood and watched."

Diana closed her eyes. Against her lids she could see the dancing flames. She heard the girl crying. How horribly Sarah must have cried. And the father, staggering back, burned, defeated. But mostly she could see the boy, the young George, helpless and watching.

She opened her eyes again. Group Captain Somers seemed to be waiting for something, though she had no idea what. She reached across the table and laid her hand on one of his. To her surprise, his skin, though age-spotted and wrinkled, was soft and supple like the finest leather.

"What more could you have done?" she asked. And when he didn't answer, she added softly, "You grew up to be a brave man. You know that. Just think of all those bombers you flew . . . the times you were shot down."

Group Captain Somers covered her hand with his other one, as though they were playing a hand-stacking game. "You're a right fine lass," he said. "My Elspeth will be glad to have you for a playmate come home time."

Diana doubted that, but still she nodded and smiled gravely.

*

By the time the conductor called Lincoln, Diana had settled so deeply into the clacking rhythm of the train that she had difficulty rousing herself. Group Captain Somers had been silent for a long time as well, but when Diana stirred, he straightened up and stretched vigorously.

"I expect she'll be waiting for us there," he said.

"Your daughter? But how will she know where we went or when we'd be getting back?"

He shrugged. "She knows. She always knows."

Of course, Diana thought, *the spies*. Would the spies know about her as well? And would it be better for her or worse if her mother had been able to learn that she was with the Group Captain? If her mother had found out, she wouldn't have been quite so worried, at least not for so long. Also, though, she would have had more time to move from being frightened to being angry.

"What'll we do?" Diana asked.

"Do?" The train was pulling into the station, and the Group Captain stood, adjusting his jacket. "We'll take a ride home. That's what we'll do. A body gets tired of trains and buses. Dolores will bring the car."

Diana peered out the window at the platform as the train jerked to a stop. Sure enough, a small, dumpy-looking woman stood beneath the platform lights with the girl Diana had seen that morning, Elspeth. Diana's mother wasn't there, though. Diana checked the entire platform, and her mother wasn't waiting anywhere.

She pointed to the pair, and the Group Captain leaned closer to the window to look.

"Never mind," he said. "She may chew us up, but she'll have to spit us out again."

"What's left of us, anyway," Diana said. She was suddenly tired, quite numb with fatigue. She no longer had the slightest idea why she had gotten involved in this expedition. She couldn't even remember anymore why it was that she hadn't wanted to go to

Lincoln with her mother that morning.

The two of them made their way down the aisle and descended the metal stairs of the train. They walked resolutely toward Mrs. Graham and Elspeth, though it was hardly necessary to do so. The Group Captain's daughter was bearing down on them like a tank, throwing a barrage of words ahead of her as she came.

"You foolish old man!" she was crying. "What do you think you're about? Running off again . . . and with somebody else's child! You could get yourself arrested behaving that way, and it would serve you right!" Her voice seemed to drown out the roar of the departing train, but unlike the train's noise, her volume didn't diminish.

"You'll be the death of me yet. I know you will. Why, my poor old mum must be spinning in her grave, seeing the way you've come to be. I don't know what to do with you! S'truth!"

Diana looked at Elspeth, who had followed silently in her mother's wake. Elspeth returned the look, her expression radiating something so like hate that Diana was stunned. Why would this girl hate her? She didn't even know her! And wasn't it Elspeth, after all, who had gone off and left her grandfather behind for Diana to deliver home? Not that the two of them had exactly made it home.

Deliberately, Elspeth turned her gaze from Diana to her grandfather, and when she did, her face changed entirely. It softened and her eyes shone with what could have been tears.

Despite what the Group Captain had said, about Mrs. Graham having to spit them out again, he didn't seem to take the chewing well. He stood with shoulders rounded and head bowed, much as he had stood in Regent's Park, receiving the barrage of words as he might have borne the lashings of a whip. Diana wanted to stop the woman's shouting, but she didn't know how.

Mrs. Graham stopped upbraiding the Group Captain long enough to lay a hand on Diana's shoulder. "Are you all right, luv?"

"Of course. I'm fine. Just fine." Diana turned a little, shrugging so that the hand fell away. "Group Captain Somers took very good care of me," she added pointedly.

Mrs. Graham shook her head, clucked her tongue. "Your mum's at your house now, sitting by the phone in case you called. I told her they called me from the station to say my dad was reported on the train with a bit of a girl. It's lucky that I met her out looking for you. And lucky that Elspeth knew the two of you were together. Even so, your mum's been quite beside herself."

Diana tried not to think about her mother, about what she had been through . . . and what was left for Diana to go through herself. Right now she had the Group Captain's daughter to deal with, and she certainly wasn't going to stand here and let Group Captain Somers take the entire blame for their expedition.

"I wanted to go to London, to meet Lady Di," she explained, "so your father took me." She glanced at the satin rosette drooping against the Group Captain's lapel and decided not to mention that he had expected to receive the Victoria Cross as well. "We met her, too. The Princess, I mean."

Elspeth pivoted and walked away a few steps, her movement as deliberate as it was rude.

Mrs. Graham merely sighed and, without acknowledging Diana's explanation, resumed her attack on her father. "At least we didn't have to send out the police this time. That's a blessing, I suppose. But I'll tell you, old man, I'm going to lock the doors, and you're not going anywhere. Not anywhere at all. Not even down to the Tempest for your pint."

She put an arm around Diana. "Poor little 'un," she said, more softly now. "You must be worn to a frazzle." And she began gently to propel Diana toward the station door.

It was almost more than Diana could bear . . . the stream of angry words directed at the Group Captain, the sympathy toward her, her mother's absence, her own fatigue. For the second time that day, she thought she was going to cry, just start blubbering in front of the Group Captain and his daughter, in front of this hateful girl.

She dug in her heels to keep Mrs. Graham from pushing her further and turned to face the woman. "He's a hero, you know," she said defiantly. "The bravest man I've ever met. He's a veteran of two world wars, and he was shot down three times . . . in flames. Then you go and treat him like . . . like . . . like he was some little kid!"

Elspeth, who had started toward the door, too, turned back, staring.

Mrs. Graham clucked her tongue and shook her head. "It's all right, luv," she said. "My old dad, he's just filled you full of stories. You don't need to pay attention to any of that." And again she tried, with a hand in the middle of Diana's back, to move her in the direction of the door.

"Stories?" Diana held her ground. She looked from Mrs. Graham to Elspeth, who refused to return the look, and back to Mrs. Graham again. "What do you mean . . . stories?"

"I mean none of it is true." Mrs. Graham fussed with her father's coat collar as she spoke, brushed back his hair as if she really wanted to rearrange what was inside. "It's all an old man's dreams, that war stuff. Nothing more."

Group Captain Somers didn't appear to be listening. His hand had crept up to stroke the red ribbon on his jacket, and he seemed to be watching something going on inside his own head. His daughter might have been talking about someone else, someone he had never met.

Diana stared, but she couldn't get her tongue moving to challenge Mrs. Graham or to ask any kind of question.

"He never even flew," Mrs. Graham continued. "He was a mechanic, a 'penguin' the boys called them. He worked on the engines back at base. He was too old in the Second War for piloting, and he was just a boy in the First. He could have gone to that one — boys as young as him did. But his father had been hurt real bad in a fire on their farm, so he was needed at home."

Diana was stunned. Not either war? Group Captain Somers hadn't fought in either war? That wasn't possible.

She turned to him. "It's a lie," she said. "Please tell me it's a lie!"

But Group Captain Somers returned her gaze and said mildly, as if the whole subject were of very little consequence, "You're right. It was a lie. All of it I told you."

"That's not . . . ," Diana gasped. But then she stopped. *That's not what I meant*, she had started to say, but what difference did it make what she had meant? It couldn't be more obvious that just now Group Captain Somers, Mr. Somers, whoever he was, had told her the truth and that everything up until now had been a story, an old man's dream as his own daughter had said.

Diana turned back to Mrs. Graham. "I'm sorry." She enunciated carefully to get the difficult words out. "I guess I was pretty stupid to believe any of it."

And then, without further prompting, she headed for the station building. She passed the ticket checker without even bothering to show her stub. When she reached the parking lot beyond, she stopped and took a deep breath.

It had been raining in Lincoln, too. The night

shone, sweet and clean, and the streetlights cast glistening reflections on the wet pavement. Diana hesitated on the curb at the edge of the parking lot. Where could she go? There were only a few cars in the lot, but she didn't know which one was Mrs. Graham's. She didn't want to get into a car with these people anyway, but she wanted even less to walk the eight or more miles back to Coleby . . . even if she could have found her way.

Out of the corner of her eye, she saw Elspeth emerge from the station. Now she would be able to see which was the right car, though she wasn't going to get in until the others had appeared as well.

Elspeth didn't go to the car, though. To Diana's annoyance, she walked right up to her and stopped by her side. "He's not daft, if that's what you think." She said it fiercely, the words a clear challenge.

"Of course not," Diana agreed, looking her straight in the eye. "He just lies."

Even in the light from the streetlamps, Diana could see Elspeth's face darken. She said nothing, but her fists doubled, and Diana's own fists clenched in response. *Let her try something,* she thought. *Just let her try!*

Behind them, Group Captain Somers and Mrs. Graham emerged from the station.

"There they are," the Group Captain called cheerfully, as though nothing at all had happened. "I expect the two of you to be right proper playmates now."

Elspeth said nothing. She simply turned and headed

for an ugly little orange car on the other side of the parking lot.

Diana followed slowly, staying ahead of the Group Captain and well behind Elspeth. Disappointment welled inside her. She couldn't tell, though, whom she was most disappointed with. The Group Captain, his quarrelsome granddaughter . . . or herself.

11

DIANA WATCHED Elspeth and her grand-
father move toward their front door. Elspeth's grandfather shuffled across the cobbled walk, clinging to
Elspeth's arm as though, without her support, he
might fall. He hadn't even said good-bye when he had
gotten out of the car. It was as though he had forgotten
Diana was there.

"I'll walk you home, luv," Mrs. Graham said, turning from watching the pair, too.

"There's no need," Diana replied, starting off, but as
she expected, Mrs. Graham came along with her, anyway.

"Thanks for getting my old dad back on the right
train," she said. "I'll warrant he didn't do that on his
own. He's quick as can be when it comes to going off,
but he always gets muddled when he tries to reverse
himself."

Diana nodded, a kind of mute *you're welcome*,
though she knew the thanks were undeserved. This
time, Mrs. Graham's father probably wouldn't have
gone anywhere in the first place without Diana's encouragement and help.

There were no streetlights, and the village was dark

beneath a moonless sky. When they stopped in front of the stone cottage where her mother was waiting, however, there was enough light seeping from the windows for Diana to see the concern in Mrs. Graham's round face.

"Maybe I'd best go in and help you sort things out with your mum," the woman said. "I could explain how he can be, how once he gets an idea into his head it's hard to turn him around."

"No," Diana said, and then, not wanting to be rude, knowing she had been terribly rude in the train station, she added, "Thanks, though."

Still, Mrs. Graham waited, as though she expected Diana to change her mind. Finally she said, gently, "I'd be pleased to look after you when your mum's at her teaching. Tell her that, would you? And tell her, too, that I'll see to it nothing of the sort happens again."

"I'll tell her," Diana agreed, though she wasn't sure she intended to. It would probably be better to have to follow her mother around the college all the time than to be stuck in the same house with Elspeth day after day.

"He doesn't mean to make trouble," Mrs. Graham said. "He just . . . comes and goes, you know?"

"I know," Diana said.

Mrs. Graham nodded, as though something was settled between them, and started down the walk. Halfway to the gate, she turned back. "We're right pleased to have you here, Diana. Both of you."

"Thanks," Diana said, but still she stood waiting just below the front steps for Mrs. Graham to reach the road. There would probably be an explosion when she opened the door, and she didn't want any witnesses. After Mrs. Graham's solid back and dark plaid head scarf had dissolved into the night, Diana climbed the steps to the front door.

*

She found her mother sitting at the dining room table, her hands folded in front of her. It was strange seeing her mother sitting there doing nothing, looking as though she had been doing nothing for a long time. Diana seldom saw her when she wasn't engaged in some kind of activity — reading, correcting papers, preparing a meal, eating. Even when her mother slept she made it look like something important she had to do.

"Hello," Diana said softly. "I'm back."

Her mother didn't answer. She simply sat there. Her hands held a wadded tissue. Diana could see that there was a box of tissues on one side of her and a small crumpled pile on the other. When she stepped closer, she also saw that her mother's eyes were red-rimmed and swollen.

It was strange to think that Mom had been crying. Over her.

Diana cleared her throat. "I'm sorry," she said.

"Why?" Her mother's voice, when it finally emerged, was pinched and raw. "Why, Diana?"

Diana didn't know how to answer. In fact, she didn't

know what the question meant. Why was she sorry? "I . . . I . . ." She pulled a chair out from the other side of the table and sat down. She folded her own hands but kept them in her lap. "I didn't mean to go off like that. It just . . . just happened, I guess."

"Just happened." Her mother repeated the words dully, without inflection, but still there was something in her tone that made Diana want to take them back. She didn't have any idea, though, what she might have said instead.

She tried again. "He . . . Group Captain Somers . . . Mr. Somers, I guess he is. He's not a Group Captain really. When I mentioned about wanting to see Buckingham Palace . . . well, he'd been wanting to go, too . . ." She examined her mother's face, then looked away again. "He told me we'd be back in time for tea. That means supper here, you know. He was going to meet you when we got back. He was going to tell you that he'd look after me while you worked. There's a law here, you see . . ." But she decided against finishing that.

"And so you went off with him," her mother said. "You met this strange old man and you decided to go to Lincoln with him and then all the way to London, no less. As if nobody had ever taught you anything."

"He didn't hurt me! He's a nice old man, a grandfather."

Her mother sighed, deeply, and Diana felt the sigh along her spine.

"That's not the point, Diana. He was a stranger. You knew nothing about him. And you were supposed to stay here. If you didn't want to come into Lincoln with me, you *knew* you were supposed to stay here."

Diana nodded miserably. Of course. She knew.

And then, to Diana's profound astonishment, her mother began to cry again. Not just tears, real sobs. Her face crumpled and her mouth dropped open, twisted to one side, and her shoulders heaved. The sounds that came out were like the tearing of strong cloth.

"Mom," Diana said. And then, half standing, urgently, "Mother!"

But her mother waved her down again, then covered her face with her hands. She spoke through her cupped hands and through the choking tears. "I was so worried. I was frantic. I don't know when I've ever been so frantic."

"I was all right," Diana said. "I *am* all right." Though she knew that saying it helped nothing now.

Her mother cried for another minute, then drew a tissue from the box next to her, wiped her face and blew her nose. That tissue joined the pile, and she pulled out another, though the tears had mostly stopped. She straightened her back and took a shuddering breath. She seemed to be getting ready to speak, but then she didn't. Diana wished she would go ahead. She wished she would yell at her, even. She couldn't think of anything her mother might say, any punishment she could come up with that would be worse than the tears . . . or the silence.

Diana couldn't look at her mother as she waited. Instead, she studied the swirling grain of the table in front of her. Mom had told her the night before that the table was walnut. She had pointed out that it was very old and very beautiful. She had said it was a privilege to be able to live, even for a year, with such old, beautiful things.

Last night, Diana hadn't thought it a privilege at all. She had said she preferred their table at home. The one her mother didn't bother protecting with placemats. The one Diana had scratched years ago crashing her Matchbox cars, so that her mother always talked about refinishing it, though she never found the time.

After a long silence, after Diana had a chance for a very long look at the table, her mother finally spoke. "Maybe," she said, "I should let you go back."

"What? Go back? Home, you mean?" Diana was incredulous.

"If you don't want to be here . . . with me, if it's going to be," her mother blew her nose again, "like this, maybe it would be best. For both of us," she added, almost as an afterthought.

Go home? Diana's head was spinning. Her mother was willing to let her go home? *Best for both of us*, she had said. That meant best for her mother, too. That meant her mother didn't want her here anymore.

Before Diana had a chance to think about what she wanted, she found herself pleading, as if staying were the privilege. "I'll never do anything like that again," she said. "I promise!"

Her mother looked at her with a steady gaze Diana could almost return, but not quite. "I know you won't," she said, "but I've been thinking. You didn't want to come in the first place. You made that," her mouth twisted into a sad smile, "abundantly clear. Maybe it was selfish of me to insist."

"But . . . but . . ." Diana felt as though she had just stepped off the edge of the earth and there was nothing beneath her feet. No gravity, even. Just the vacuum of space. "But what would I do? Where would I stay? I can't stay by myself for a whole year." (Though that had been one of the plans she had proposed before they had left Minneapolis.)

Diana's mother answered without looking at her. "Meghan's mother made an offer once. She said you could stay with —"

"With Meghan?" Diana leaped to her feet. "And you never told me!" She leaned halfway across the table, her voice dangerously loud. She could see her mother wince.

"Why?" Diana shouted. "Why didn't you tell me? Meghan and I talked and talked. We *dreamed* about it, about my staying with her, about being like sisters. I wanted that more than anything in the whole world, but you made me come here . . . with you. You said I had to." And Diana repeated herself the way her mother had when she had first come in, "Why?"

Her mother pushed back in her chair, but she held Diana's gaze for a long time before finally lowering her eyes. Her fingers moved precisely and methodically, tearing the tissue she held into jagged little flakes.

Diana remained standing, waiting.

"I suppose because I wanted you here . . . with me." Her mother seemed to be speaking to the pile of torn tissue. "You'll be grown so soon, and gone, I didn't want to lose this year with you."

The enormity of it, the unfairness of it, almost took Diana's breath away. "But you're never here!" she exploded.

Mom looked up, her eyebrows arched. "Never?"

Diana knew how her mother felt about words like *always* and *never.* She said they made an argument unfair . . . and untrue. So Diana said grudgingly, "Well, almost never. You have to go to work most days." Still she wasn't going to let her off the hook. Meghan's mother had said Diana could stay with her, and her mother hadn't even told her about the offer or given her a choice.

"Yes," her mother agreed, "I have to go to work most days. I'm responsible for providing for you."

Diana straightened up, crossed her arms over her chest. "You don't have to work every minute . . . just to provide for *me*!" She hated it when her mother did that, used her as an excuse for what she wanted to do anyway.

Mom pushed the paper aside and faced Diana squarely again. "You're right, Diana. I work as much for myself as for you. And I know I work harder than is good for either of us. But" — she looked down once

· 105

more, dismissing Diana and all her arguments with a faint shrug of her shoulders — "you don't know what it's like."

How Diana hated that! The ultimate adult argument, *You don't know what it's like.* And how could she know, how could anybody know anything unless they were told? She sat down slowly, gripping the edge of the table with both hands. "Then tell me," she commanded.

Her mother seemed surprised, and at first Diana thought she was going to refuse, that she would tell her she was too young to hear. But she didn't. Instead, after another silence, she began speaking in a tight voice. "I know I work too hard, that my hours are too long. But sometimes I think that if I let up, even for a minute, someone will come and take it all away. It's as though I have to be good, better than anybody else, just to stay even."

Diana stared at her mother, incredulous. "Take what away?"

"My job. Our home. The food on our table. Everything you and I have."

Diana still didn't understand. "But you're a professor. You've got a Ph.D.! Nobody else's mom has a doctor's degree!"

Her mother smiled wryly. "There are others of us out there, moms with doctorates. Sometimes all applying for the same job. And because I was just finishing my degree when the divorce came, the judge refused to give me any child support from your father. As if you and I could eat a Ph.D., wear it."

"But you've always had a job. Even when I was a little baby, you were working. I thought it was what you wanted to do!"

Her mother turned her palms up, as if she were helpless to explain further, but then she went on anyway. "It is. I love my work. But I'd love being home with you, too. And I've desperately wanted a job that would be secure, one I could settle into for a while and not have to keep moving."

"I hate moving," Diana said vehemently.

Her mother nodded. "I do, too. But I haven't had any choice. I've been pretty good at finding short-term positions, filling in for someone on sabbatical for instance, or positions without tenure, with no guarantee of being hired the next year. Maybe after I do this exchange, when we go back to Minneapolis . . ."

"We'll be able to stay?"

"I hope so. I can't promise, though."

"If you had stayed married, everything would have been easier." Diana couldn't help saying it.

Her mother's chin shot up but then came down again, more slowly. All she said was, "Some things would have been easier, Diana. Not all."

"At least I would have had a chance to know my father, if you hadn't left him. I'm the only kid I know who's never even met her own father."

Her mother looked at her, steadily, without speaking, and at first Diana thought that she was going to go completely silent again the way she had been at first. Finally, though, she did reply. She said, "Diana, I didn't take you away from your father. *He* left *us*."

Diana stared. She was stunned. Why hadn't she been told before? It was her life. He was her father. She had a right to know!

"Why?" she demanded. "What made him leave? Did you drive him away?"

Her mother replied so quietly that Diana had to lean toward her to make sure she caught every word. "He left," she said, "because you were born, and he wasn't ready to be a parent."

Diana sat perfectly still, letting the information reverberate inside her. Her father hadn't wanted her. Not only now, but even in the very beginning. Hadn't wanted her to be born. That was the thing she had been feeling all these years, the terrible thing her mother had been hiding. Part of it, anyway.

Probably her mother hadn't wanted her either. How could she have? She, Diana, was the reason for the divorce, the reason Mom had to work so hard, even the reason they had to keep moving.

"Were you sorry?" she asked finally, slapping the words down on the table like cards certain to lose. "That you had me, I mean?"

"No," her mother answered, her voice as firm as stone but a great deal warmer. "Never."

Neither of them said anything more for several minutes, and finally Diana stood, slowly, almost reeling with fatigue.

"But I can choose now, to stay here or go back and live with Meghan? It's for me to decide?"

"It's for you to decide," her mother said.

Diana allowed her gaze to travel around the room. She studied the dark, old furniture, the massive fireplace, the thick, plastered walls and deep-set, leaded windows. It all felt so strange still.

She let her scrutiny rest on her mother, who sat there, her hands folded next to the pile of torn tissue, her face wiped smooth of all expression.

"I guess I'll need a little time to think about it," she said softly.

12

"DO YOU WANT to go for a walk?"

Diana looked up from her breakfast plate in surprise. "Don't you have to go to work?"

"No. I called this morning to tell them I wouldn't be in today. I figured you and I needed time to get some things settled."

Diana nodded. "Okay." And then she added as an afterthought, in case her mother was forgetting that she had promised the decision about staying would be hers, "I haven't decided yet, though ... about whether I'm going home."

"That's all right. It's too important a decision to be made quickly. A year is a long time."

"When we were coming here," Diana said, giving her mother a teasing smile, "you told me a year would be short."

Mom laughed. She stood, picking up her empty plate. "I guess it's all a matter of perspective. For me, it would be a long time to be separated from you."

Diana took the last bite of her fried egg. It was funny; the orange yolk looked different, but it tasted the same as eggs at home.

"Come on," her mother said. "We'll put the dishes in the sink to soak. Then you can show me what you discovered about this place yesterday . . . before you went off to explore other lands."

So Diana showed her mother around Coleby. The sun had emerged at last, transforming the village so that it looked like something out of a brilliantly colored painting, the kind you might see in a fairy tale book. Diana didn't know why she had thought of the stone houses as gray. They were more cream-colored actually, and they seemed at home where they stood in a way American houses seldom did, almost as though they had grown up out of the land itself.

Diana also noticed for the first time that the houses all had names instead of the less interesting numbers buildings had at home. Theirs was called, appropriately enough, "Wayfarer's Rest."

She took her mother into the ancient church, and the shadowy coolness was a pleasant contrast to the emerging warmth of the sun. The church wasn't like a tomb as she had thought at first. Rather, it felt dark and mysterious, the kind of place a person might almost expect to meet God.

As they emerged into the sunlight once more, Diana spotted Elspeth and her grandfather coming along the street on what was apparently their traditional morning outing. Diana started to turn the other way, but a voice boomed out, stopping her exactly as it had the day before, "Well, good morning. And who might you be?"

Diana stood still, studying her feet and waiting for her mother to respond. Obviously, Mr. Somers was speaking to her mother. But when Mom nudged her instead of replying, she looked up to see that he wasn't addressing her mother at all. He was looking directly at her.

A faint chill tingled the back of her neck, but she replied, looking into the cloudy blue eyes, "Why . . . I'm Diana Baldwin from Minnesota." She avoided looking at Elspeth, who was avoiding looking at her.

"We are honored to meet you, Diana-Baldwin-from-Minnesota," he replied, beaming. "This is my granddaughter, Elspeth Graham." Elspeth was looking off down the street, her face flushed and her lower lip held tightly between her teeth. Clearly she found her grandfather's behavior acutely embarrassing. Or was she simply afraid that Diana might be making fun of him? Maybe all her crossness the day before had been caused by her feeling protective of her grandfather, whom she obviously loved.

"And you must be Diana's mother," Mr. Somers continued, turning to Mrs. Baldwin. "I'm pleased to make your acquaintance." He held out his hand. "You have a lovely daughter."

On again, off again, his daughter had said. Diana couldn't tell whether he had shifted gears and now knew who she was or not. He was still wearing the red satin rosette on his lapel. Did he even remember what it was supposed to be?

"Come along, Granddad," Elspeth interrupted. Her

voice was gentle, almost wheedling. "You don't want to make me late again, do you?"

She had taken hold of his free arm, and he released Diana's mother's hand and said, tipping an invisible hat as he backed away, "Another time perhaps, Mrs. Baldwin. My granddaughter, here, is always in such a hurry."

He moved off with Elspeth toward the walking path, and Diana and her mother stood, watching them go.

"He seems like a nice man," her mother said. And then she added, smiling, "A bit forgetful, maybe."

"A bit," Diana agreed, beginning to walk again. After a moment she added, "He told me he served his country in two world wars. He wasn't even in one of them!"

"Maybe he was telling things the way he needed them to be."

"I suppose so," Diana said. She remembered saying to him, *You grew up to be a brave man.* But of course, he didn't believe he had. In any case, he had never had a chance to prove it to himself . . . except in the dreams he manufactured.

"I'm through with dreams," she said.

"Why?" her mother asked.

"They don't change anything."

Her mother shrugged. "Except the most important thing."

Diana shot her a startled look. "What's that?"

"The dreamer."

Diana stopped at the entrance to the Viking trail and turned back to face her mother, confusion and exasperation struggling with one another. "Why do you say that? You *hate* it when I dream!"

"I hate it when you let your dreams, or somebody else's, take you off to London without my even knowing where you've gone." Her mother reached out as though to touch her, but then let her hand drop instead. "And I guess I get aggravated sometimes when you aren't paying attention. But life without dreams would be pretty poor. Don't you think?"

Diana didn't know what she thought. She turned and started along the path.

They were walking single file, so when her mother spoke, the words drifted up from behind. "Diana, you will make friends here, you know. If you decide to stay, that is. Dolores Graham says Elspeth is just your age."

Diana didn't respond to that. Adults always thought finding friends was easy for kids, that if another kid was the same age nothing more was needed. But she had never once heard her mother come home filled with enthusiasm because she had just met another thirty-eight-year-old woman.

Diana climbed over the first stile and stepped down into the pasture on the other side. A calf gamboled out of her way, stiff legged, tail held high. Several older, more sedate cows moved off more slowly, then stopped to gaze at the encroachers with reproachful eyes.

"Hi, cows," Diana said, but none of them answered. "Do you suppose English cows moo with an accent?" she asked.

Her mother laughed and stepped down next to her. "They probably say, 'Haloo, luv.'"

Mom took the lead across the pasture. The silence between them was comfortable now. Diana wondered vaguely what she was going to decide to do.

To go back and live with Meghan . . . for a whole year! It sounded wonderful, but what would it be like not to see her mother for all that time?

They came to the next stile, which was farther than Diana had reached the day before. She followed her mother over it, descending on the other side into a field of intense, yellow flowers. It was like the fields she had seen from the train. The golden blooms were astonishing, the color in the sunlight so dazzling that it almost hurt her eyes to look at it. A breeze passed across the field, making the yellow blossoms sway and flicker.

"I've never seen anything like it," her mother said, her tone hushed as though the brilliant flowers might startle at the sound of her voice.

Elspeth and her grandfather were ahead of them on the path, about halfway across the field, but that was all right. It was, after all, as Diana had reminded herself yesterday, a public path.

Then she heard again that too-familiar name. "Sarah," Mr. Somers was calling. "Sarah!"

Did the old man sometimes mistake Elspeth for his long-dead sister, too?

But when Diana looked, she saw that he wasn't calling to Elspeth. And he wasn't turned back toward her either. He had moved off the path and was running, stumbling through the blazing field toward a stone wall on the other side.

"Sarah!" he cried again, his voice high and wavery. "Fire!"

Diana looked around, confused. Where? What fire?

Then she realized. Perhaps it was some trick of the sunlight, but Mr. Somers thought the lustrous, yellow bloom, extraordinarily vivid this morning, was flame. He thought the entire field was burning. And this time he wasn't going to stand and watch.

"Sarah. Where are you?" The old man tripped and fell, and then he was struggling to his feet again, still crying, "Sarah!"

Diana looked to Elspeth to take charge. He was her grandfather, after all. She must be used to such spells. But Elspeth seemed too deeply caught up in her grandfather's confusion and pain to do anything. She stood where she was, her face twisted with anguish, reaching helplessly, silently, toward the retreating figure. Whether this had ever happened before or not, Elspeth obviously didn't know what to do.

Diana turned to her mother then, but her mother, her competent, efficient, take-charge mother, only returned her look, her eyes wide with bewilderment.

"Sarah!" The old man was beginning to circle frantically. His feet tangled in the bloom, and he fell again. This time he stayed down, beating the blazing flowers with both hands.

Diana had been able to help yesterday. Mrs. Graham had said her father didn't normally return on his own from one of his excursions.

She took a few steps from the path into the shimmering flowers. "Here I am," she called. "Over here." And then keeping her back to her mother's gaze — pretending, in fact, that no one was there but Mr. Somers and herself — she added, loudly, "Please, save me!"

Mr. Somers staggered to his feet again, looking frantically in every direction until he spotted Diana. "Sarah!" he bellowed, and then he was running toward her, his face shining more brightly than all the radiant blooms.

Diana stood perfectly still, waiting to be rescued in the old man's dream.

*

Diana and her mother watched Elspeth and her grandfather making their way back across the pasture.

"I'm proud of you," her mother said quietly.

A deep warmth glowed in Diana's chest. Then her mother had seen; she had understood. Still, she replied, "He won't remember. Tomorrow . . . or the next day, he'll probably have to live it all again."

"He must be a brave man," her mother said, "to keep on the way he does."

Diana nodded her agreement.

Elspeth's grandfather had begun to climb the stile at the other end of the pasture. He stepped up with one foot, brought the other to join it, then repeated the process like a very young child. Elspeth was hovering close behind. When he had descended to the other side, she was at the top. She hesitated there, then turned back, just for an instant, and gave a quick, bashful wave.

Diana waved back.

Her mother waited until the pair had disappeared from view before speaking. "I hear there's a castle farther down this valley," she said. "Do you want to see if we can find it?"

Diana was surprised to hear there was a castle so near, but she nodded and moved out in front of her mother on the path once more. "There must be lots of castles in England," she said over her shoulder as they approached the next stile.

"Lots," her mother agreed.

"And I suppose it would take most of a year just to see half of them."

"I'm sure it would." Her mother's voice was tentative, hopeful.

Diana took her mother's hand to help her over the stile. The hand was warm in hers, both soft and strong, and her mother kept a tight hold even after she had stepped down.

"I think that'll be fun," Diana said. "Don't you?"

Her mother drew in a long breath, squeezed Diana's hand in wordless agreement, and then let go.

Diana fell into step beside her.